the PERSONA

AIRSHIP 27 PRODUCTIONS

The Persona
"Enter—The Persona!" © 2016 Michael F. Housel

Published by Airship 27 Productions
www.airship27.com
www.airship27hangar.com

Interior illustrations © 2016 Art Cooper
Cover illustration © 2016 Shannon Hall

Editor: Ron Fortier
Associate Editor:Gordon Dymowski
Marketing and Promotions Manager: Michael Vance
Production and design by Rob Davis.

ISBN-10: 0-9977868-1-7
ISBN-13: 978-0-9977868-1-1

Printed in the United States of America

10 9 8 7 6 5 4 3 2 1

"Enter—The Persona!"
by
Michael F. Housel

Enter—The Persona!
PROLOGUE

(Brink Town, NJ…July 1938)

Black robed people gathered about the tombstones, their hoods pulled around their heads, shadowing their faces. Some leapt over the arched formations as if playing leap frog, while others wore grim expressions, choosing either to stand on the sidelines or pace between the grassy aisles.

Poised next to a large, pillared mausoleum, upon which the surname Mansford was etched, Jon Pickwick, the High Monarch of the Ministry of Chaotic Command, conversed with his immediate subordinate, High Disciple Carmine Pascale. They spoke softly, but their exchange was distinct enough for others to hear, including a woman whose thick, gray curls protruded as she crept down the nearest moonlit pass.

"But I mapped the entire area, with ample room to spare," Pascale argued, his round face contorting, "not that such should matter. I was under the impression, Jon, that this *thing* we're to conjure thrives on blasphemy, or at the very least, a general sense of disorder."

"So true," said Pickwick with a frustrated yank of his Van Dyke beard, "but we still have to watch what we designate, Carmine. We don't want any coffins disinterred. It will only make it harder for us to maneuver, complicate matters in the little time we've been allotted."

"You're terribly pessimistic for a High Monarch," said Pascale and pointed to a small, claw-like spike lodged not far from the closest stone. "See? I left a decent perimeter and measured the circumference, meticulously based on what your old, Germanic text describes."

Pickwick strolled toward the spike and inspected the area.

"It should be wider…much wider," he corrected. "Based on your haphazard design, I'll have to layer the solution a foot farther beyond the outer rim."

He then looked past Pascale, catching the gaze of his flock, before settling on the gray-tufted woman.

"Fear not, brothers and sisters," he called. "We are about to commence the proceeding." He then knelt, grazed the grass. "First, we must anoint the area, so that the spell will take proper hold." He grinned. "Oh, yes, the soil feels most susceptible tonight."

He stood and pulled from out his long, deep pocket, a brass bottle, unscrewed its cap and proceeded to trace Pascale's shaky outline, moving from spike to spike, dropping the gooey substance outside the impression, while chanting under his breath in what sounded like Pig Latin, but was really just an indignant form of hopeful murmuring.

As the fluid was dropped, the men marched inward, the women gyrating on the outskirts, though all made their way toward the Monarch, their expression respectful but surly, their garbled purrs mimicking their leader's.

Pickwick returned before the mausoleum, while Pascal followed, positioning himself against the pillar nearest the farthest left of the tomb.

Their guru then raised his hands, his palms aimed at the ground and announced, "The time has come to defile all that is pure, to set forth our vessel of confusion and doubt upon this sickeningly sacred land and once and for all, tear it down."

A sense of incomparable doom fell over the graveyard, which the devilish troupe welcomed, its members bowing their heads, humming in contemptuous contemplation.

The soil then rumbled and with one, great whistling swoosh, several spikes shot upward, rocketing into the sky, then rained down, inserting themselves near the flock's feet, somehow leaving the catalysts miraculously unscathed.

"Look, look," Pickwick exclaimed. "It's happening. It's happening."

Overjoyed, the members, including even those who had acted previously reserved, leapt over the monuments, bumping into one another like the flipped bearings of a pinball machine, the revelry troubling Pickwick, for he knew their job was far from done.

"Steady yourselves, brothers and sisters," he scolded, watching the soil sadly settle. "We must refocus on what dwells below...."

Though most members obeyed, others continued to swagger, forcing Pickwick to dart toward them, cluster them closely, when...

From the distant, weather-worn work house, a hard pounding came, a flutter of light spilling from the side window, a blind being raised.

The silver-haired caretaker regarded them from behind the glass, mouthing obscenities, the side of his hand pounding the pane.

Unsettled by this unexpected turn, Pickwick turned to the gray-haired woman, then pointed accusingly at Pascale, snarling, "You assured me, there was no one else here..."

"The last two workers left hours ago," Pascale charged. "I checked the building thoroughly, Jon...was certain it was empty. I just don't see how..?"

Pickwick slugged Pascale across the jaw, knocking him backward, and as his subordinate caught his balance, the others looked for direction.

"We must retreat," Pickwick bellowed, scampering forth, energetically waving his members onward, as the older woman followed alongside. "Hurry…hurry. We'll finish this later; revise our plan, make it better."

The caretaker then bolted from the house, shaking his fist, screaming at the top of his lungs, "You've no right to be here, you lousy cretins. I'll call the police, you hear? I swear."

Pickwick and his flock moved into obscurity, venturing past the open gates, piling into their scattered vehicles, and though they were discouraged, they realized they were far from through. Pickwick's passionate presence alone assured them of that.

Somehow, someway, the Ministry of Chaotic Command would fulfill its goal. Far sooner or later, Brink Town would crumble as planned.

(I)

Ned Stark flung the rubber hand from the cardboard box, pretending it had leapt of its own accord. He struggled with it, while bending the fingers in such a way to make them latch onto his throat. He then swiveled his waist, causing the ruddy wrist portion to rock back and forth: a most surreal sight, considering the backdrop consisted of benched Charlie McCarthy knockoffs and framed advertisements for skin caps and fake dog excrement.

"Get it off me," Stark gagged, his arms flailing. "It's…it's choking me."

Michael Mansford stoically regarded the demonstration: his usual style when observing the latest prototypes. Generally, he would rub his jaw or tap his foot, sometimes slick back his black hair, insinuating approval or disapproval with a trite wink or groan, and in the end, his opinion almost always went contrary what was conveyed.

Stark, being a tad hefty, wheezed and yanked the hand from his neck. "Well, what do you think, boss?"

The young codger drummed his chin. "It's clever," he confessed, "but will it fit all necks?"

Stark bent the fingers backward and fanned them outward. "Sure will. It's actually larger than a normal hand and has loads of wires inside to ensure durability. With a little tinkering, one can even latch it onto one's arm or wrist. It's a doable, one-size-fits-all format, Mike."

"And the production," asked Mansford, "can be completed exclusively at our Brink Town facility?"

"Yep, right at the good ole' Esoteric Incorporated's manufacturing plant: no outside strings attached. In fact, our equipment is geared to accommodate every aspect of production."

Mansford folded his arms. "If it's not too much to ask, Ned, could you demonstrate the gag one more time?"

"Okay," Ned said with a shrug, reattached the hand to his neck and swayed. "How's that?"

Mansford exhaled, hesitated and then said, "Sure, I think it has obvious potential. Whip up an initial batch of two hundred. We'll distribute in the tri-state area, see where it goes from there."

Stark stopped shaking and sighed. "Great, I'll get right on it."

A strident rapping then struck the door.

"Uh…yes?" asked Mansford.

The door swung open, revealing his old, silver-haired friend Phillip Sutton, his gait cold, determined.

Sutton had worked in his earliest years as a dock foreman at Esoteric; then for a decent duration at Mansford Fisheries and Supplies, and now in his pre-golden years at the Mansford Blessed Tidings Cemetery, just outside Brink Town: a family establishment, which like the others, the thirty-year-old Mansford now owned and operated.

In any event, Mansford respected Sutton because of his no-nonsense nature, and therefore when the older man buffered himself against Mansford's desk, the young entrepreneur assumed the worse.

"What's wrong, Phil? Vandals again?"

"Worse than that," said Sutton, his eyes shifting to Stark, who still toyed with the hand. "This time I fear it's damn pagans."

Stark lowered the hand, choked back a laugh, to which Mansford shot a disapproving frown.

"Well, at least I think they were pagans, Druids…whatever you might want to call them," said Sutton as he slipped on the defensive. "They were wearing robes and were humming up a storm. A good number of them even leapt over the tombstones like it was May Day or something. I wouldn't have believed the audacity of it, Mike, if I hadn't seen it with my own two eyes. Really, it's a good thing I didn't leave when I was supposed to; just happened to have dosed off after Fred and Peter left." He frowned. "As you know, I don't particularly like hanging at home, with the wife's nagging and all."

Mansford nodded, then interjected, "So, what did you do about these… uh, pagans, Phil?"

"I was too dumbstruck to do anything at first," Sutton said, "then got real ticked off, pounded the window, chased them off…called the police."

"Oh," said Mansford, "and what did the police say?"

"Not much," said Sutton. "They sent Jack Murphy, the beat cop. Big deal."

"I know Murphy," said Mansford, "at least for the sake of small-talk exchanges."

"Well, he's sure good at that…small talk. He jotted some notes for his report, said he'd keep an eye open, and that was that. Thanks for nothing, you know."

"Perhaps for the time being, that's all he could do," Mansford expressed. "On the other hand, you have noticed other examples of vandalism. You think it's the same hooligans?

"No doubt in my mind," Sutton confirmed. "And what unnerves me most is we're not talking kids here, Mike. These weirdoes were adults, and one of them, kind of familiar in some respects, and a real wicked looking bastard, at that, was tossing around this weird goo. Can't figure out what it was, but it sure smelled funny. Most of it's since bled into the dirt."

Mansford took a moment to ponder the matter, then glanced at Stark.

"Ned, why don't you let us tend to this?" Mansford suggested. "Do whatever's necessary to get that item into production. If I have to sign any paperwork, just slip it under my door. Sound good?"

"Sure," said Stark and tossed the hand into the box. "I guess I'll touch base with you later, then."

"Now you do that, Ned," said Mansford, walking him to the door. "I appreciate all the work you've poured into this. Marketed right, I'm confident the Creepy Clutching Hand will be a veritable smash."

He then led Stark to the hall, offered a sincere smile and shut the door, spinning around to eye Sutton.

"I must say," said Mansford with a grim pout, "I don't like this idea of people disrespecting the dead. Least we not forget, Phil, my parents are buried there."

"Along with your grandparents," Sutton added, "not to mention a slew of aunts, uncles and several second cousins, twice removed. Also if word gets out of this to the public about this activity, people will start looking elsewhere to lay their loved ones to rest."

"I hear you," said Mansford. "Now, if memory serves me correctly, you're off the next couple days, right?"

"Yeah," said Sutton, "but I wouldn't mind covering extra shifts. I've really got nothing better to do."

"Well, to be perfectly honest," said Mansford, "I've been meaning to stop by to sift through some of our recent invoices, and since I keep odd hours, anyway."

"To be honest, I really doubt those goofballs will be back so soon, now that they've been spotted. Besides, Fred and Pete will be there the whole stretch while I'm off. I know they're a couple of jugheads, but they'd do well enough to keep their eyes peeled."

Mansford laughed, patted his friend on the back. "All the same, I really should have a look around. Tell me, when exactly did you catch these characters in action?

"About half-past midnight, give or take. They were probably there a while beforehand, of course. Looked like they got in through the east gate. It was left open, thanks to either Fred or Pete, but the intruders could just have as easily climbed any section of fence. Not every spot is spiked along the top."

"Gotcha," said Mansford, "To start, I'll set my sights on tonight. I'll use your little room in the back of the work house when I'm not milling about. As I recall, it's a cozy space."

"Heck, it's even got a radio."

"Excellent," said Mansford, placing a hand on his friend's shoulder. "I think we're set." He then led Sutton to the door. "Now, you don't worry about a thing, Phil. You have a couple nice days off, go fishing or camping, whatever suits your fancy, and when you get back, I'll let you know what transpired…if anything."

With a shrug, Sutton went his way, appearing at least content that Mansford had taken his concern to heart.

Mansford, however, was more than just concerned. He was incensed. He had no tolerance for sects that dared trample upon other's sacred traditions, and his worry over such had elevated severely during the past few years through newspaper articles and newsreels. Though such groups were few and far between, he realized the influence they wielded and believed it would only take an incident or two to elevate them into the mainstream: case in point, Germany's mounting Nazi movement. Now, that was one weird (and dangerous) cult.

He pulled a couple Mansford Publishing cultural-taboo texts from the shelf, deciding to take them along to the work house. He was sure he only had to reference "graveyard rituals" or something to that effect, and from there could pretty much ascertain who these culprits were and maybe even unravel where they were hiding...

(II)

However, to pinpoint such ghoulish pastimes proved more daunting than Mansford had anticipated, with most topic-related information focusing on Burke and Hare. He could only conclude that the group Sutton had chased was a haphazard pagan or satanic offshoot. On the other hand, its members may have been little more than masquerading drunks. It wouldn't have been the first time Mansford had encountered such shenanigans. He had witnessed many acts of blasphemous revelry in his college days.

Discouraged, he tossed the texts to the side and after a lonesome hour or so, decided to engage in a verbal brawl with Fred and Pete, who just happen to stop by to chide him on not putting his time to better use. The criticism was justified. After all, he had sacrificed a cozy night in his penthouse suite with the ever enchanting Penelope James, heir to the Powder-Puff Beauty Salon franchise, hoping to spot something unlikely to occur, and even if such did, Fred and Peter would have been there to catch it.

Why did he push himself so? It was as if he had to prove himself, or at the very least over compensate for being well-to-do...perhaps. Then again, he recognized the innate drive that pushed him to identify anything that seemed wrong. The roots of evil had to be snipped, he told himself, or else the consequences could prove insurmountable.

In any event, the exchange with Fred and Pete soon grew redundant, and they agreed to depart to make their rounds. This gave Mansford ample time to leaf through the invoices, but of course, the exercise was fruitless, and so he turned on the radio, and let some Brahms wash over him, every so often peeking out the window to the area where Sutton claimed the offensive proceedings had taken place.

He repeated this act several times before resigning the effort and dozing, content to spend the rest of the night in his comfy chair, when out of nowhere, several virile screams erupted. He assumed he was dreaming, but sprung up all the same, shooting toward window, but spotted nothing out of the ordinary and cursed his overactive imagination. He sighed and settled back into his spot, only then to hear two more intense yells, and this time dashed outside.

"Is that you Fred?" he shouted, looking from side to side. "Pete...you okay?"

A sense of dread curdled the air, bolstering the humidity to the point where Mansford perceived an eerie haze rolling across the grass.

He rubbed his eyes, hoping it would go away, but when it remained, he decided to march into it, making his way toward the mausoleum. Its large, ornate doors were pushed inward.

"Fred?" he repeated. "Pete?"

He saw the latter hunkered on the left, bound and gagged, his red-hair tussled, his right eye blackened. The poor man was unconscious. He then glanced to the right and saw Fred also unconscious, restrained in similar fashion, his bald head bruised, his bottom lip shattered.

"Son of a bitch," Mansford muttered and to check the extent of the men's injuries, edged forward when something hard struck his head. He winced, spun around and gazed into Pascale's hateful eyes, then down at the crowbar protruding from out the man's thick, robed cuff.

Mansford reached up, hoping to muster the strength to fight back, but then slumped downward, his consciousness fading.

"Let the fool be," a woman called from a far. "We must move fast, before this chance slips."

"Yes," a man answered, from about the same locale. "Without question, every sign does point to the here-and-now. Hurry, Carmine, hurry. Time truly is of the essence."

"All right, Jon, all right," Mansford's attacker groaned. "I'm coming. I'm coming."

Mansford attempted to raise his head, but the gesture proved in vain, as blackness succumbed him.

●●●

When Mansford awoke, he was surrounded by hooded people. A few feet from where he lay, Pickwick waved Pascale inward, who now cradled a petite blonde, attired in a sheer, white night gown, her limbs flaccid and flailing.

Pascale then passed the young woman over to the apparent leader, a tall, bearded man, while those gathered hissed an indiscernible chant.

"What in God's name?" Mansford groaned, suspecting the whole scene a bad dream.

Pickwick rocked the woman in his arms, in synch to the deepening chants, before placing her at the heart of a foggy circle. He then patted the ground and smiled.

With arms outstretched, palms aimed downward, he declared: "Forgive us, Great Beguiler for having falsely enticed you. We should not have fled, but rather faced our aggressor and culminated your summoning. Nonetheless, we have absorbed your latest request and wish to fulfill it, and so to compensate for our shameful hesitation, we offer you a sacrifice as virginal as the first fallen snow. Defile her in symbolic jest if you wish and rise among us to take your rightful place in a world that begs to be torn asunder."

The spectators elicited one last, discordant murmur and stiffened.

From his pocket, Pascale pulled a small spike, tossed it to the bearded man, who in turn, hoisted it like a knife, then lowered his arm, creeping toward the girl, who stirred and moaned.

Unnerved by the implication, Mansford shot up and jaunted across the grass, but when the ground started to rumble, he paused, teetering.

In a mad rush, those assembled bolted, including their apparent, frantic leader, leaving the woman to roll and writhe. The strange flock then hunkered behind a queue of larger stones, giving Mansford the impression that the phenomenon was perhaps expected, or in the very least, premature. Had one of these lunatics miscalculated a detonation? After all, earthquakes were uncommon to Brink Town.

Whatever the cause, Mansford was not about to let the woman lie, and despite the hazardous circumstances, continued toward her.

The onlookers gasped and pointed as he skidded to her side, slipping one hand behind her head, the other just above her derriere. However, as he lifted her, the ground shook further.

Pickwick's eyes met his, bristling of anger and surprise, while dirt spouted a wide, dusty halo above the lower haze, disorienting Mansford.

"It's coming," Pickwick bellowed, smacking fist into palm. "It's coming."

The earth then rocked with such intensity that Mansford lost his balance, dropping the woman, who opened her eyes and regarded him in confusion.

He reached down to pull her back up, when the ground buckled, cracked, insinuating some great force rammed upward.

Then from out a swirling hole, the head of a large black beast emerged, its four, beady eyes shifting in all directions, while its four muscular arms broke from various spots about the dirt, propelled by four long, leathery, hands, upon which four clawed fingers gleamed.

"Praise all that is blasphemously insincere," the bearded man exclaimed. "The Great Beguiler has risen."

In a matter of seconds, Mansford watched as one of the creature's four taloned paws rose over the now panic-stricken lady. Mansford moved fast, however, grabbing her ankles and yanked her toward him, just before the monster could stomp her.

Mansford skidded to the side, leveraging himself to reach back down, when as his luck would have it, he tripped, tumbling into an unforeseen, craggy crevasse, where he dropped several additional feet, bracing his heels to each side of the coarse chasm, hoping he possessed the dexterity to ascend.

Meanwhile, he watched the creature pause, arching its head back like a gun hammer, exposing its slimy incisors, expanding its throat like that of a giant frog to emit a most blood-curdling croak, the thrust of which caused the dirt walls to shake and slip around Mansford, spiraling him downward.

He anticipated death, or some form of severe physical calamity, but as the seconds lengthened, his perspective changed.

His brain tingled; his body felt soft and intangible. From below, an ebbing light reached out to him, demanding that he enter it, but before he could contemplate its blinding drawl, he was well within its luminous heart.

(III)

Mansford looked up, a dirt ceiling arched over him, tinged in a deep, yellow glow.

Around him, small, orangey fires smoldered from out bronze cauldrons in various points around a dirt floor.

A man in a black robe stood nearby, but unlike those of the cemetery, his cloth appeared spun of silk, beneath which a frilly white shirt protruded, the collar peaking Dracula-like from behind his neck, and his face...well, he had no face, unless one considered zooming swirls of smoke and two, beaming hazel eyes, a face.

"Who are you?" Mansford asked, sitting up from a hovering, feathery cot. "What...what is this place?"

"As for my name," the entity replied in a soft, florid voice, "Mister

Surrogate will suffice, for my true identity, as you can surely infer from my mystical disguise, must for now remain a mystery. As to our location, let's call it a temporary station, one fashioned especially for us, for this special moment in time."

"If you say so," said Mansford, rubbing his temple. "Say, maybe I have died," he mused, "and perhaps you're...oh, God, no. I'm far from a saint, but I've never done anything so vile as to end up..."

Surrogate laughed. "That's ever so true, Mister Mansford. In fact, I'd say you're one of the very few tried-and-true characters I've come across in my ventures, and as far as devils go, the entity above better fits that legendary label than I ever would."

Surrogate then gazed upward, craning his neck, revealing skin that was rich, blurred white, watching as a few dusty particles trickled down to his crown. "I certainly hope this structure holds. We're not allotted much time, I'm sorry to say."

"Time for what?" Mansford asked. "Please tell me, why am I here?" He looked about, trying to pick up some clues. "Everything that's occurred feels out of whack, far more a dream than reality."

Surrogate raised a gray-gloved hand and extended his index finger. "Ah, I would greatly differ on that point, Mister Mansford. Whether above or below, what you're experiencing is as real as any reality can aspire to be, particularly mine." He folded his arms across his chest. "Unbeknownst to the damned Beguiler and his poor misguided sheep, I forged this sector with the sheer power of my mind, snuck it right in under their noses, then when the moment was right, sucked you into it. In this way, we could more readily converse. Oh, I'll reinstate you to the surface soon enough, but not before I give you an essential device to guide you through the ensuing days."

"All right, said Mansford with a huff and leapt up, looking Surrogate straight in the eyes. "I'm assuming I'm here to help somehow, and if that means saving the young lady, I'm more than game. So, go on, then. Spill the beans."

"Indeed," said Surrogate with a contemplative sigh. "First off, you should know that, to fulfill your mission, you will need to purge all confusion, all deceit: those traits that the Beguiler and his followers most desire for the sake of control."

"Oh...okay," said Mansford, discouraged by the continued ambiguity, "I see. Well, I'll have you know, Mister Surrogate, I've never had much success keeping a clear head."

"You gravely underestimate your abilities, Mister Mansford," said Surrogate, shaking a finger. "Haven't you ever wondered why you're so meticulous? Some say you're neurotic, eccentric...quirky, that you have your hands in way too many lofty schemes, but you know as well as I, you have the talent to work on several, intricate levels. You attract not only the good, but the bad. By the very fateful construction of things, the Beguiler knows this as well, and it only goes to reason why the ghastly creature transmitted rebellious thoughts to those robed charlatans: just another means to set the odds against you. In order to rise, the Beguiler needs patsies: people perplexed enough, unclear enough, to believe chaos guarantees fulfillment; the direct opposite of you."

Mansford shrugged. "In all honesty, it's probably just as well I stay clear of them, and as for that creature, I think it's suffice to say mere chit-chat is likely to appease it. By any other name, a beast is a beast."

Surrogate shook his head, sending wistful plumes from his cheeks. "It's not through discussion that you'll combat the Beguiler, Mister Mansford, but through thoughts, ideas...images. You'll absorb the creature's madness, its blind rage, chew it up and spit it right back at the thing. Truly, Mister Mansford, it's the most effective way to bring the beast and its subordinates to their knees."

"Sounds simple enough," Mansford quipped. "But, uh, how exactly do I master this spitting-it-back technique?"

Surrogate shifted his eyes to the side and waved Mansford over to a small, golden table, atop which appeared a concave formation, concealed by a swirl of white silk.

"Through this," said Surrogate and yanked the cloth away, bending his body in such a way to block Mansford's view of it. He then turned, lifting the item with delicate precision. "You will wear it, and through it, your senses will become amplified, and if properly tuned, perhaps even take such to supernatural heights."

Mansford's gaze fell upon a pearl-lustered face...a mask, in fact, with eyeholes wide and round, rendered with porous nooks and meandering cracks, its lips finely chiseled and pronounced. To each side, just above the cheekbones, were two, small golden bolts and protruding from the inner back of each side, the hint of a thick, black band. Mansford was at a loss for words, finding himself drawn to the odd, shimmering persona.

"Legend claims," Surrogate continued, aware of Mansford's enchantment, "that the mask was melded from scrapings shaved straight from Heaven's pearly gates: a magical guise to help one identify the good and bad in all people, and for the latter, the means with which to offer suitable comeuppance." He stepped closer to Mansford, positioning the mask toward the subject's face. "Here…put it on."

Though the temptation to do so was overwhelming, Mansford hesitated, for the prospect seemed too bizarre to entertain, but the mask's pearly sheen proved magnetic, and before he had any viable inkling, he had stretched the soft band around the back of his head, letting the mask's smooth, inner surface suction his face.

"Splendid," Surrogate exclaimed, clapping and rolling his eyes. "It fits like a charm." He backed up, swaying his smoky head to and fro. "Oh, yes, you look quite regal…so divinely intimidating."

Though Mansford could not see the effect for himself, Surrogate's words captured how he felt…royal and strong, magnanimous, too.

More dirt trickled from above, and from there, the beast's hateful roar vibrated down into the chamber, shaking it, starting to compress it.

"There's no time left to loose," Surrogate cried, raising his hands. "For now, you have enough information to commence your crusade. Please, you must leave…must return."

Mansford embraced his guide's words and began to ascend, his body once again tingling, growing soft and gossamer as he rocketed through layers of dirt.

The night sky appeared, along with a hint of the towering creature, its head bowed, its jaws unhinged, staring cock-eyed at the girl, and Mansford's molecules reassembled…

(IV)

It was his face…or more rather, the mask…that formed first. Mansford knew this, for he watched the shiny persona reflected in each of the monster's piercing orbs.

It reared up, turning its hideous head, one of its four, cumbersome feet pushing the crouched and trembling woman away from it. Mansford could now see the extent of the beast's height: at least sixteen feet tall, eight foot wide. He also noticed the deft way it maneuvered its mighty legs over the ground's indentations, which connected to the slighter ones, creating a jagged circle.

From the side, Mansford saw the bearded man lift his head from behind a crossed-tipped stone, his face crinkling of awe and fear. Mansford's limbs then took form. He felt the fine fabric of his clothes wrap around his skin and raised his hand, an accusing finger pointing at the man.

The sinister guru grimaced, then bolted, his followers sprinting behind him, while the creature lumbered over an opposite queue of stones, into high shrubbery, merging into the darkness, grunting for a spell, with an ominous silence following.

Mansford stiffened, his mind not his own, until his thoughts and memories rushed forth. More by accident than plan, he looked down at the hunkered young lady, who also appeared on the verge of flight, but hesitated, as if to determine whether she were friend or foe.

"It's all right," he uttered, his voice reverberating from behind the mask. He reached back, pulled up the strap and revealed his face. "It's me...the man who tried to help you." The humid air moistened his cheeks. "Are you...all right?"

"Yes, I think so," she whispered, too strained to speak any louder. "You... you said you tried to help me?"

"Indeed," said Mansford, "from those strange people...and that ghastly thing." He stepped closer, the mask dangling, poised like an emblem upon his chest. "Do you know these people...what may have caused all this?"

She shook her head. "I'm sorry," she replied, "I don't. I was in bed, sleeping. That's all I remember."

Mansford heard Pete moaning, followed by Fred. He slipped the mask onto his arm like a gauntlet and leapt into the mausoleum. He then loosened their gags, nudged their limbs free.

"Holy Moses," Pete choked. "What the hell happened?"

"We got zonked over the head," said Fred. "That's what happened." He stood and reached down to help his friend up, then to Mansford said, "Those were probably the same nuts Phil chased away last night."

"Of course they were," said Pete, dusting himself off. "Who else would they be?"

Intrigued by the exchange, the young lady gadded toward them, cuddling herself, self-conscious of her sheer attire. Fred and Pete scanned her, though more out of nervous spontaneity than any salacious disrespect.

"Oh," said Mansford, "this unfortunate girl was intended as a sacrifice to that horrid creature. You boys did see the creature...didn't you?"

"Creature?" Fred said. "What creature?" He chuckled. "You joshing us, Mike?"

"No, he's right," said the young lady, her voice now shrill and succinct. "I saw it with my own eyes...big, black, with several arms and legs." She

"Are you…all right?"

closed her eyes, cringed. "It was like something out of a nightmare...but ever so real. I swear."

Mansford, hoping to appease her troubled state, ushered her back onto the grass, where he now noticed more than several stones tipped and skewed and asked, "What's your name, Miss? Do you live around here?"

"My name's Stacey...Stacy Standish," she said. "I live with my parents, not far from here...in Primrose Square."

"Ah, Primrose Square," he said, "nice part of town." He offered his hand. "I'm Mansford...Michael Mansford." He smiled. "I'm also a resident of Brink Town."

She appeared confused, though shook his hand. "You mean you're *the* Michael Mansford...Michael Mansford, the tycoon? Oh, my."

Mansford laughed. Considering what she had just gone through, it seemed peculiar she would get excitable over something, at least in comparison, so trite.

"Well, Miss Standish," he said with as much humility as he could muster, "I can't say I've quite reached that prestigious level yet, though I am working on it." His tone then turned earnest. "Nonetheless, the issue at hand is, I'm uncertain what to do about our present predicament." He considered the matter, though felt an inexplicable impulse to throw caution to the wind. "The better part of wisdom tells me I should simply drive you home, you see, and yet..."

"Yet what?" she asked, as if being accused of some wrong.

"Well, regardless of how outlandish the details," he explained with a grin, "I'd venture the police should be informed of what's transpired." He looked back at Fred and Pete, who were peering from out the mausoleum. "Tell you what, Miss Standish. The boys can call the police, and I'll take you home. If the authorities will wish to question you, they'll find the means." He grazed his arm, tracing the pearly persona. "All the same, what's happened is just so fantastical, so..."

"Mystical," she chirped.

"Yes, mystical, sure...and jarring," he added, reaching into his pocket for his keys. "My Packard's parked near the south-side gate." He slipped his hand into hers. "Perhaps we can chat on the way, if you don't mind. I must admit, there are a few things I'm yet curious about."

"That's fine," she said, allowing him to pull her along. "As long as I can ask you a few of my own."

Mansford agreed, and despite Fred and Pete begging them to wait, across the cemetery they trekked, anxious, confused and for whatever odd reason, elated.

(V)

"So," said Mansford, "I know the basic direction to Primrose, but at this point, onto what street do I turn?"

Standish shrugged. "Well, it's hard to say."

"Hard to say?" Mansford laughed. "Come now, you've forgotten how to get to your home?"

"On second thought," she confessed, "I'd rather not go. Just because a gal lives with her parents doesn't mean she finds it pleasurable. I really don't relish the idea of explaining things to them, and for that matter, what in the world would I explain?"

The absurdity of their intent struck Mansford hard, enough so that he almost broke from his euphoric state, contemplated returning to the cemetery, waiting for the police, but in glancing at Standish's angelic face, his inner drive dictated the terms, abetted by the persistent, ineffable tingling that inundated his arm, where the mask still remained.

"Considering what you've just experienced, my dear," he reminded her, hoping a little logic might prove persuasive, "I'd think any place would look just heavenly in comparison."

"You don't understand," she said. "They'll question why I left the house. I'll have you know, my father gets terribly enraged when he thinks I'm insincere." She reached over, grabbed Mansford's forearm. "Please, Mister Mansford, please…don't make me go there."

"Very well," said Mansford, realizing the extent of her conviction, "but precisely where should I take you? A motel, maybe?"

She paused, then suggested, "Why not to your place? I'm sure I'd feel so much safer there, and when the police need to question me, I'll be right there to converse. It might even legitimize our leaving the scene."

The prospect of bringing such a fetching, young vixen to his penthouse enticed Mansford, perhaps more than was respectable. Could he trust himself? For that matter, could he trust her? No matter, it was probably worth the risk.

"Okay," he consented, "but only on one condition. You level with me. You must have some inkling how you got to the cemetery. You must have some notion who took you there. I want you to come clean, Miss Standish… no more talking in circles."

Standish appeared a tinge offended, but then consented. "Okay, I'll tell you want I know," she said, "but much of it's still all rather hazy." She cupped her knees and grimaced, as though to force the details from her mind. "I was sleeping. I know that much. Someone got into my room. I think it was their second-in-command, though I truly didn't discern his face. It sensed it was him, though. I remember him leaping atop me, putting this foul rag under my nose. It made me dizzy...made me faint. I remember that much. Then the next thing I knew, those hooded cretins were gathered all around me, murmuring. I thought I might be dreaming, but sensed an unshakable danger in the air and, well, you figure out the rest, Mister Mansford,"

"When they were murmuring," Mansford asked, "could you make any sense of what they were saying? Did you, by chance, catch any of their names?"

"The man who entered my room...I think his name might be Carmine, or something close to that. The one in charge, his name's John or Jim, or at least I think I heard this Carmine fellow call him something along those lines. I heard some woman jabbering, too, but I don't recall her addressing anyone by name."

"And you're positive you hadn't seen any of these people before, not even in passing?"

"Certainly not, Mister Mansford."

"Hmmm," Mansford pondered. "Seems odd they'd pick you. I mean, Blessed Tidings is a good stretch from Primrose. You're pretty, my dear, which as King Kong so astutely taught us, would make you a prerequisite for the sacrificial section. Nonetheless, there are lots of pretty gals these fiends may have picked."

"Maybe they spotted me on the street, going home...maybe even where I work."

"Where do you work, Miss Standish?"

"The library on most days," she said, "sometimes at the Lincoln Theater, though mostly on weekends, when the kids come to catch the movie serials, cartoons and such. Anyway, it's not like I'm invisible."

"What's your religious affiliation, if I may be so bold?"

"My mother's Catholic, my father Protestant, or so they claim, though I have my doubts. They fight a lot in a general sense, but religion is never the topic at hand."

"And what of you? Any interest in weird cults?"

"Beyond my reading about the Aztecs and Mayans in school...no."

Mansford drummed the steering wheel. "Well, I sure can't figure it out. I guess the police can handle the finer details, the ins and outs, as it were, but of course, when it comes to the actual supernatural elements... that creature, in particular...I don't know what to say." He paused, contemplating his own circumstance. "I wonder where that hideous thing may have gone? Something that large can't stay hidden."

"Hopefully it's disappeared," Standish said, "vanished like a puff of smoke, back to wherever it came." She shook her head, shivered. "Let's hope, anyway...right?"

Mansford veered off the main strip, onto a tree-trimmed road, which led to a small, but elite section of town called Stately Manors, in the heart of which his apartment complex stood.

Standish, noticing its looming lights flickering into view, asked, "Mister Mansford, do you, by chance, have some inkling whom these culprits might be? I mean, with all due respects, sir, they did choose your cemetery."

He smiled at her shrewdness. "My hunch is they simply needed someplace sacred to defile. Blessed Tidings was probably the most sensible pick: lots of religious symbolism, going back many years, and of course, there's ample space."

She reached over again, and this time tapped the mask, but retracted her fingers and blew upon them.

"Ouch," she said. "That sure smarts." She pouted, and her tone turned terse. "Say, what is that thing anyway?"

Mansford paused, uncertain if he should share what he had experienced, but figured it best to keep matters mirthfully vague. "Let's just call it a little ace-in-the-hole I stumbled upon."

"If you say so," said Standish.

Mansford zoomed into the driveway and pulled into his designated parking place, close to the angular, art-deco entrance. He then leapt out, shot around the other side and escorted Standish from the car and into the building.

Charlie, the gaunt, elderly night guard, was milling about the lobby, his back to the doors, and to avoid any idle chit-chat, Mansford took advantage of the moment, whisking Standish into the elevator, pressing the button several times to the top floor.

As the door shut, Charlie waved, but upon spotting the young lady, frowned, raising an urgent finger, which Mansford dismissed.

"Shouldn't I register?" Standish asked. "That man seemed rather concerned."

"Oh, ole' Charlie just wants to shoot the breeze," Mansford explained. "Given the chance, he'd bend your ear for a good hour or more. At this stage of the game, I'm just not in the mood."

After they ascended, they exited into a short, orange-lit hall surrounded by diamond-shaped mirrors along each wall. Mansford shot over to the sole door at the farthest end, unlocked it, reached in and flicked on the light, then with an inviting smile, waved her inward.

Standish nodded and stepped into a museum-like expanse, amazed and perhaps a tad intimidated by the odd gamut of it, for ventriloquist dummies and marionettes populated the far wall-shelves, while on a long bench beneath the curtain-drawn windows, yet another dead-pan batch was queued.

Between the puppets, framed movie posters of Universal horror films, like "Frankenstein", "Dracula" and the "The Invisible Man", hung with reckless abandon, and when she turned, she beheld a dozen curio cabinets containing art-deco ladies of varying sizes: all slender, curved and in various forms of undress.

"My," she remarked with pretentious glee, "I'd have never thought."

Mansford shut the door and said, "I guess you were expecting something more, well, posh. So sorry to disappoint." He walked past her, sliding the mask from his arm and slipping it into his desk drawer. "In case you haven't heard, I'm known for my eclectic taste."

"I'm fine with it...really," said Standish. "It's just that, at first, it's all a bit...well, overwhelming to take in."

Mansford laughed, but his guffaw was cut short when a female voice from the bedroom beckoned: "Mike...Mike, is that you?"

Mansford froze. "Terrific," he muttered, realizing all too late what Charlie tried to convey.

"Mike?" the woman called again. "Mike...why aren't you answering me?"

The sound of a body bouncing of the bed followed, then the scampering of bare feet, revealing at the threshold, a short-haired brunette, wearing a gown so sheer it put Standish's to shame.

"Dear goodness," the brunette gasped, tears filling her eyes as she sprung back into the room.

Mansford shot Standish an apologetic glance, listened as the closet door creaked, the clanging of a hanger. When the woman reappeared at the doorway in his best, cotton robe, her arms were crossed, her glare unforgiving.

"So, I see," she snipped, "working late at Blessed Tidings you said. We'll, it's a good thing I planned this pleasant surprise." She scanned Standish with disdain. "I assume you found this strumpet on the high-school beat. Well, I must say, she looks as worse for wear as you, my dear. What were you two doing, rolling in the hay?"

Standish was far too in awe to be insulted. "You're...you're Penelope James," she squeaked. "I read about you all the time in the socialite postings." She fluffed out her hair and straightened her attire. "I even visited your salon the other day." She extended her hand. "Gosh, this sure is a pleasure."

James ignored it with a flutter of her lashes and quipped, "I'll refund your money, sweetheart. The Jean Harlow look is so passé."

"There's no need to get derisive, Penny," Mansford scolded. "This poor girl has been through a most harrowing ordeal." He straightened his collar, brushed his sleeves. "And so have I. It wouldn't hurt to slow up and not jump to conclusions."

The brunette strained a vicious chuckle and whined, "I've spent my lost drop of sympathy on you, Michael Mansford. Father was right. You're nothing more than an overindulgent man-child." She pointed about the room, as if discharging a Tommy gun. "Look at this place, would you? It's like an oversized carnival booth. Well, I need a man with sophistication, class, one who's loyal to the core, and you, Mister Mansford, most assuredly don't fit that bill." She wiped her hands and spun back into the bedroom. "No siree, Buster...I am through."

She tossed the robe out at him, and after a few mind-numbing minutes (wherein Mansford and Standish were left to exchange awkward glances) re-entered in her expensive green gown, matching shoes, pocketbook and a silver, diamond-studded necklace, the latter of which Mansford had given her that past June.

With her head cocked to the ceiling, she charged past them, halting before the door, only then to ask, "Well, aren't you going to reason with me to stay?"

Mansford shrugged. "Maybe it's best you just sleep it off, Penny. I'll call you sometime tomorrow...okay?"

"Oh, don't bother, you cad," she screeched and shot into the hall, slamming the door behind her.

"Geese, I'm sorry, Mister Mansford," Standish said, wringing her hands. "If I had any inkling I might put you in a jam..."

"Ah, don't worry about it," Mansford replied, emitting a relieved sigh.

"Oh, and please, let's cut the formalities." The tension left his face. "Call me Mike."

"All right," she consented, "as long as you call me Stacey."

"Swell," said Mansford and stepped over to the bedroom. "Well, Stacey, beyond being a bit disheveled, the bed's obviously open for occupation… if you're interested."

Standish's eyes widened.

"Oh, no, I didn't mean to imply…" Mansford stammered. "I meant, you should get some shut-eye if you can, and believe me, the bed's considerably more comfortable than the couch." He glanced at his watch. "And perhaps I should head back to the cemetery. The police are surely there by now."

"Sure, I understand," she said. "Though I must confess, I'm probably still a little too wound up for rest."

"It only goes to reason," Mansford agreed, but proceeded to gesture her into the room, "but do try your best, all right?"

She complied and sat on the edge of the bed, pushing her derriere against the clumped blankets and sheets. She looked at him in such a way that made him want to stay. Indeed, Penelope was right. She sure did resemble Harlow.

"I'll be back soon," he promised, finding the fortitude to pull himself away.

He then darted out the room, but just as he began to exit, a police officer greeted him, with hand poised to knock.

"Officer Murphy," Mansford exclaimed. "Well, this is a fortuitous surprise. In fact, I was about to return to the cemetery. I asked my men to call your station about a most perplexing incident that occurred on the grounds tonight."

"That's why I'm here," Murphy confirmed, squinting over Mansford's shoulder, into the room. He was a young fellow, close to Mansford's age, affable enough, but with a slight swagger that surfaced when he commenced any inquiry. "I was on break from my beat at the Java Shop, indulging at my scheduled time, when the call came in. I was told you might head home, if I got it right. Nonetheless, looks like I was right, of course." He looked Mansford over, his brow crinkling. "So, sir, what gives? Is this connected to Mister Sutton's report from the night prior?"

Mansford glanced back into the living room, at his desk, considered the significance of the mask, as well as the lovely lady in his bedroom. "Uh, well, in a way it does. You're very intuitive, officer." He tapped his foot, trying to garner his thoughts. "Anyhow, the whole thing's rather difficult to explain. Perhaps, it's best we just head back to Blessed Tidings, and you can see things for yourself." He smiled. "I'll be happy to drive."

"That'll be great," said Murphy. "Been on my feet for nearly six hours now. To say the least, my dogs are killin' me."

Mansford pushed his way into the hall and locked the door behind him. He then led the officer toward the elevator, intent on keeping any speculative causes and effects minimal. The cemetery's condition would speak for itself.

(VI)

"I'll pull right up to where it happened," said Mansford, his headlights swerving round the bend, stone after stone swaying into view like a queue of dominoes. "Like I said, you can see for yourself."

Murphy craned his neck, anxious to do just that. "Okay," he said, "you point it out to me, Mister Mansford."

The mausoleum appeared, along with Fred and Pete, who faced the opposite direction.

"Yep...there are my men," said Mansford. "They'll fill you in."

However when he exited the car, Mansford was startled to find the area no longer marred by the gnarly crevasses. In fact, the ground appeared as smooth as it had before. Even the stones were stable and straight, and when Fred and Pete turned, they were unscathed: not a solitary cut or bruise.

"Say," said Mansford, dashing over to them and pointing about. "What gives?"

"What do you mean, Mister Mansford?" Pete asked.

"The damage, for crying out loud...what happened to all the damage?" He looked Pete square in the eye, waved his fingers where the man's wounds had been. "You're not even wounded. How'd you heal so fast?"

"What do you mean, Mister Mansford...heal?" Fred intervened. "And what damage? Sure, there were some kids here, but we chased them away, remember? You said to call the police, and well, so that's what I did." He glared at Mansford. "Are you all right, sir? I told you to have some coffee before you left. Liquor will mess with one's perception, after all."

"What in the world?" Mansford seethed. "What's going on? Who's put you up to this, Fred? Damn it, tell me!"

"Now, now," said Murphy, "there's no need to get excitable." He cut between Mansford and the groundskeepers, focusing on the latter. "So, there were kids here, you say?"

"Yes," said Pete, "teens, probably the same ones Phil Sutton chased off last night. You came out to inspect, didn't you? You remember…"

Murphy scratched his head. "Yeah, I sure did. Didn't see anything then, either. Still, I must say, the delinquent problem is getting worse in these parts every day. Real shame. Personally, I blame the parents."

"Hold on," said Mansford, "we're not talking delinquents here. These individuals were adults, dressed in…"

"Yeah, robes," Murphy replied. "Heard the same song and dance from Sutton. So, what is it, Mister Mansford…you two sippin' from the same hooch or what?" He leaned toward Mansford, took a whiff. "Well, you don't smell of whiskey. I'll give you that, but all the same…"

"I assure you, officer," said Mansford, "I am not in the least bit intoxicated." He again scoped the surroundings, realizing the evidence was not there to support his claims and then decided it best to try to save face. "I guess I was just…well, mistaken. I naturally assumed there was damage. Generally, that's how it goes. Delinquents are rarely inclined to let things be."

Murphy frowned and charged, "That's funny, sir…you made it sound as if I'd find something cataclysmic when we were on our way."

"Forgive me for that," said Mansford with apologetic calm, though his mind raced a mile a minute. "This cemetery's been overseen by my family for years. It's important it remain unfettered. Many people in town have their loved ones buried here, myself included. Besides, the moonlight can play tricks on one's perception. I'm obviously no exception."

"I can appreciate your zeal…and the misconception," Murphy said. "Yeah, my aunt and uncle were laid to rest here. Listen, I more than appreciate the sentiment, Mister Mansford. Nonetheless, if there's no apparent damage…"

"Evidently not," Mansford admitted, then asked, "You'll at least make a rudimentary report, correct?"

"Same as last night," Murphy said. "I'll patrol the vicinity more often, though, particularly around this hour. Trust me, Mister Mansford, sooner or later, we'll nab these hooligans."

"Very well," said Mansford. "Perhaps, I might drive you back…"

"No…no, I've enough renewed spring in my step to handle it from here," said Murphy, exchanging congenial nods with Fred and Pete. "I'll check things outside the fence before I depart…certainly can't hurt."

"Thank you, Officer Murphy," said Mansford and watched him head beyond the mausoleum. When he was far enough along, Mansford turned to Fred and Pete, quite intent to ream them out, but noticed them heading toward the work house, their motions rigid and zombie-like.

"Hold up," Mansford hollered.

Without turning their heads, they paused, but then continued onward.

"What the hell," Mansford grumbled, but let the men continue onward, figuring it best to return to his car, hoping there was some way he might find the means to contact Surrogate, but how, unless...

The mask...yes, that was the answer. Perhaps if he donned it, he might make the necessary connection, or at the very least, achieve some form of insight in the process.

Mansford hopped into his car and as fast as he could, trekked back to his penthouse.

(VII)

"I tried to tell you, Mister Mansford," Charlie explained. "She was up there a good hour before you arrived, and when I saw that little peach with you, dressed the way she was, I just knew there was gonna be trouble."

"I appreciate your concern, Charlie," Mansford said, edging into the elevator. He reached for his wallet, pulled out a ten. "Here, take this for your trouble. I really do appreciate your concern."

Charlie feigned reluctance, but took the bill, continuing to gab as he slipped it into his shirt pocket, "Yeah, you never know who might show up, considering the building's luxurious reputation. People want to sneak in here all the time. You've always got to question folks, but in Miss James' case, I didn't see the need, especially with her having her own key."

"Sure, sure, Charlie," Mansford said, hitting the button. "What could you do? For better or worse, the damage is done. Really must be going, though, my friend."

Charlie's eyes gleamed. "Oh, yeah, of course, Mister Mansford. Shouldn't keep the young lady waiting." He winked. "You have yourself a nice night now, despite that little mishap."

"Thanks, Charlie," said Mansford, as the doors shut. "Appreciate it."

As soon as he reached the top, he bolted and slipped back into his apartment, not knowing what to expect at this point, though all appeared in its proper place.

He peeked into the bedroom, saw Standish stretched upon the bed, sound asleep and with this, strolled to the desk, pulled out the mask and held it under the stained-glass lamb, watching the light cascade across its slick surface.

"Mesmerizing looking thing," he whispered, his fingers caressing the slight, meandering wrinkle across its brow. "Superb craftsmanship, too."

His fingertips tingled, and the impulse to don the mask grew stronger. A revelation then struck his head and toward the bedroom he walked. Again, he gazed at the girl, now curled kitten-like.

He strapped on the mask and beheld a soothing, amber glow engulf her…an aura, which felt pure and sincere, and above her head…if his eyes dared not deceive him…a halo.

"My word," he gasped, his voice echoing within his disguise, "It's a message, I think. The poor dear…she's virtuous, all right, in no way in league with the devilish things we witnessed tonight. Yes…yes, I'm sure of it."

He backed up, turning toward the living room, watching as the same amber glow swept over his possessions, and then as his eyes shifted toward the door, a dark figure appeared and behind his pearly encasement, Mansford smiled.

"Hello, Mister Surrogate," he said.

"Hello, Mister Mansford," Surrogate answered, his facial plumes swirling with sly mirth. "Glad to see you're testing the waters. That's a very good start."

Mansford dashed toward him. "I don't know how you got here, Mister Surrogate, but I'm glad to see you. I'm so very confused, you see. Can you tell me what happened at the cemetery, what foul trick is at play?"

Surrogate's body crackled, wavering like a burst of electricity, then he reeled a tinge before his outline reformed.

"So…so sorry about my instability," Surrogate stuttered, raising his hands, "but you must understand, as a projection, I'm sometimes limited in the way I can control my presence. Nonetheless, I sensed the urgency, and so here I am."

"And not a minute too soon," said Mansford, "Again, please just tell me what's happening."

"I know you want a to-the-point explanation," Surrogate said, "but truly, in an instance like this, even a condensed assessment would only prove wasteful. What's essential you must learn solely on your own. What you learn will resonate better that way, and as for the cemetery, if you had just taken the mask, you'd have surely seen…"

"Seen what?" Mansford asked, but again Surrogate fizzled and this time slid back into the door, in such a way that only half his body protruded from out.

"See?" said Surrogated. "Things aren't always what they seem to be. Now, do us both a favor. Start over. Take a nice stroll. I'll guide you along, but only up to an adequate point, and by the time you return, you'll have a decent handle on what the mask can do…and what of course, is transpiring."

Though impatience racked Mansford's brain, he forced himself to comply. "Very well," he consented. "Lead the way."

Surrogate formed a smoky smile, then slipped out of the door, but when Mansford opened it, the specter was nowhere in sight.

"Great," said Mansford, "so much for an adequate point."

"Pssst," Surrogate hissed, hovering before the elevator, the doors opening, as he waved. "Come on…time's a-wastin'."

Mansford followed, the hall ebbing of sunray strands as he made his way in.

The doors shut, and as they descended, Mansford warned, "Charlie's going to get a real charge out of this. You know, we won't make it so quickly out the building."

"Of course, we will," said Surrogate, "because the mask will cloak you from him."

When the elevator opened, Surrogate floated past him, again disappearing, and though this perturbed Mansford, he focused on his task at hand, and glided right by Charlie, whose gaze remained fixed in thought.

"I'll be darn," Mansford acknowledged, exiting the lobby, his heels skidding across the walkway and onto the street that led to the park. "Impressive, Mister Surrogate…but now what?"

"Continue on," the invisible agent whispered within the passing breeze. "Like I said, you'll soon see. Soon, all will become clear."

Mansford obeyed, watching the park lights beam like mini-moons in the steamy humidity, the grass sparkle as if sprinkled by golden dew.

People passed him, but whether they saw him, he could not say, nor did he care. He felt content to move unseen, his confidence building as he traveled from street to street, enraptured by his own innate drive.

Indeed, he had unraveled some higher purpose, even though at this point, its complexity remained unclear. No matter. He was on a mission, and whatever it entailed, he would fulfill it.

•••

A storefront came into view: Flynn's Schwinns. Two adolescents leaned against its front door: one with rusty curls, the other, a stubbly crew-cut. Their attire was unkempt, their actions shifty, and in the crew-cut boy's hand, a truncated coat hanger. .

"That's not gonna work, Mace," the red-head boy hissed, pressing himself upon the crew-cut boy's shoulder. "We'll never get in."

"Hush, Randy," the crew-cut boy shot back. "Give me a sec. If it doesn't work, we'll just break the stupid window." He shoved the wire inside the key hole, twisted it. "I gotta get me that bike…you know, that damn green one. Man, oh, man, is that ever the catch."

"Hey," said the red-head boy, "that's not fair. We're supposed to share. I got tired of that little girl's bike too, pal." He chuckled. "You know, I'm glad we finally sold it, though, not that there was much left of it when we were through."

Mansford's agitation rose, and before he realized it, he was halfway down the block, not so much walking as he was soaring toward the ruffians.

"Ah, there we go," declared the crew-cut boy, as the door popped open. "Hot damn." He turned to his friend. "See, I told yah…"

The crew-cut boy's eyes shifted, and his mouth fell agape. He tapped his friend's shoulder, pointed toward the approaching ghost.

"Holy smokes, Mace," the red-head boy stammered, as Mansford's iridescent face filled his pupils. "What…what the hell is it?"

"Hell if I know," said the crew-cut boy, "but we better scram."

The boys bolted, but in an instant, with seamless, supernatural finesse, Mansford was on them, reaching down, grabbing the boys by the backs of her grimy collars, his fingers prickling their skin.

Then, as if culled from their collective minds, Mansford perceived a stony sign, centered at a peaked building top: BRINK TOWN ORPHANAGE. His eyes then dipped to a sunny lot, children playing in it, including a little girl who circled about on her shiny red bike; the two boys in question darting inward, pushing her off the bike, the crew-cut boy hopping onto it, the red-head boy laughing as he clung to his friend's back as they sped off. Father Bruno, his goateed face wrought with rage, leapt from the façade, tripping down the steps, shaking his fist and hollering, as the little girl slumped and sobbed.

"We didn't mean to do it," the crew-cut boy whimpered, breaking the reverie.

"That's right," said the red-head boy. "It was just a joke. We were gonna give it back. Really, we were."

"But of course you were," said Mansford, his voice drawled and reverberating. "That's what you little cretins always say." With a sweep of his hand, he swept the door shut, clicked it locked, then lifted the boys off the ground, their feet flailing. "You sold the bike, remember? Perhaps you'd like to confess the matter with the police, or should I just drop you off at the reformatory."

"No, please, no," the crew-cut boy cried. "Neither one. We'll change our ways. We promise. Truly we will…whoever…whatever you are."

"I'm afraid it's a tad too late for that," said Mansford and propelled them both onward, his body, and theirs, moving with uncanny weightlessness. "Yes, I do believe the police station is the far better option. It's only a block away."

The boys wailed, as they continued to sail, the pavement appearing to ascend like an icy escalator, the street lights streaming like ethereal banners.

"There you go," said Mansford and tossed them both onto the police station's concrete steps, and pointed to its large, intimidating doors. "I suggest you go in, tell them what you did, but I must warn you…I'll know if you don't."

"Sure, sure," said the red-head kid. "We're going, Mister. We're going."

They then rushed up to the door, just as Murphy was exiting, garbed in casual attire.

"Whoa, there boys," he said, blocking their passage. "Slow down. What gives?"

Mansford, however, scooted off, rounding fast down the next block, where Surrogate waited, leaning against a stop sign, his face a serene blur, insinuating a carefree stance, though Mansford's intuitive powers detected otherwise, absorbing the entity's earnestness and conviction.

"Magnificent, Mister Mansford," the specter praised. "Your performance embodied the proper panache. More importantly, it appears you've left a profound impression on those lads."

Mansford stopped before him, his heels grazing the ground. "Glad you think so," he said, his cognition readjusting to something more earthly. "It was, indeed, a most invigorating sensation: so wide, so expansive, and in that vision, I sensed all the insensitivity, the spite, the sadness, as if it were my own."

"…go in, tell them what you did…"

Surrogate nodded. "When immersed in an avenging state, it's common to empathize with the victims, especially since the culprits rarely do, but in that you tasted that little girl's panic and woe, you can bet your bottom dollar, those boys did so, too."

"So," Mansford conjectured, "the mask turns me into a filter of sorts."

"Filter? Why, yes, I suppose you could say," Surrogate agreed, "but a most powerful one at that. Through the mask, emotions become accentuated… yours, as well as the participants'. The effects are also accumulative. They'll fuel you whenever you don the mask. They'll enhance your actions; give you extraordinary abilities so that you can better discern good from bad. All in all, a nice set-up for one of the right, moral disposition…and you are of the right, moral disposition, Mister Mansford."

Though the thought of such responsibility intimidated Mansford, he knew the gamut of his convictions. "Yes," he said, "I'm inclined to see what you mean."

"I'm pleased you perceive it that way," said Surrogate. "So, now that you're on board, what else might you wish to pursue tonight to further your burgeoning crusade?"

"Well…the cemetery, I suppose," said Mansford. "Wasn't that the whole point of this venture, anyway?"

"Of course," said his mentor, "but once you're there…then what?"

Mansford shrugged. "In all honesty, I don't rightly know. Perhaps you'd be so kind to guide me."

"Oh, but you don't need me," said Surrogate with a playful swipe. "I'd just be a crutch. You need only to open your eyes, prick up your ears, follow your nose, as it were, and you'll be fine. Personally, I think if you give matters a little more time to saturate, you'll be most surprised by what else you'll find."

Mansford nodded, empowered in a way he had never felt before: eager to comply, anxious to discover.

Surrogate then gave him a thumbs-up, and after a hardy, electrical spurt…*poof*…he was gone.

Mansford sighed, pondering the most efficient path to Blessed Tidings sans a car, but then decided it best just to follow the streetlights' surreal stream.

As such, an ebbing aura prevailed, beckoning him like a friend, but with the trailing sheen also came sounds: subtle at first, but then dissonant, like an overlapping of radio waves, fighting one another, containing arguments between spouses; children pleading not to do their homework;

men gabbing about finances, among other such intense devices. Some of the vocalizations were more insidious, catering to contemplated robberies, muggings and embezzlements. Others were so rudimentary they really did not warrant attention and yet they prevailed: what to make for breakfast, how much should be set aside for groceries, what movie to see that Saturday night, would a babysitter was available.

Where to begin and end with all these words and ideas, Mansford could not say, but in spite of it, he let most of the concerns wash away, leaving only the darker, more dangerous ones to linger, but even they were hard to sustain.

What surfaced was far more complex: ineffable rumblings, garbled and bestial, their underlying implications, deceitful. What intensified them was the cemetery's appearance, and it was there that Mansford believed these strange mutterings emanated.

As his soles swooshed across the ground like skates, he regarded the work house: dark and still, implying that Fred and Pete had since departed.

He glided toward the front gates. As expected, they were locked, and though he had no qualms to climb them, he also realized there was no need, for via an unconscious command, he floated upward, then descended over the top to touch the enclosed grass.

The overlapping chattering continued funneling ever louder into his ears, as the mausoleum protruded from a roll of fog, along with the surrounding, beckoning white stones.

Behind this veil of idyllic stability, where all seemed even and hard, markers revealed themselves once more as tipped and skewed. The encircling trench also reappeared, still smoldering, and about such, peculiar activity stirred.

Monsters were gathering about, which resembled the behemoth, but of various sizes and heft: some as tiny as cats, others more-or-less dwarfish, some as tall as any regular man. They all grunted and groaned, bending down or sprawling upon the dirt and grass, plunging their claws into a batch of open canisters labeled: PROPERTY OF BLESS T.

Watery white paint slithered down their fingers, which they slapped onto random chunks of cardboard culled from torn boxes they had nabbed from the dumpster out back, many of which were already fastened to branches and sticks. But why? What was the intent?

Mansford sensed their blind determination, their anger and urgency, as they robotically twitched, as if without wills of their own, their thoughts twisted, drained...misconstrued.

One of the dwarfish variations bounced up, cocked its head, aware of Mansford's approach and croaked. The others turned, their beady eyes glistening, their slobbering jaws agape. Mansford's presence unnerved them, or at the very least, his glowing face.

They snorted at one another, grabbed their finished products, some kicking over the cans, scampering off into the bushes, but Mansford remained on their trail, cutting through the air, tracking the shiny sweat off their backs as they headed toward the fence.

They slid...or rather, broke...through the bars like billowing smoke, the cardboard flapping onward through the bars in their tenacious grasps. Mansford continued to track their smeary, translucent shapes which streaked through the streets, mingling with minds (or so Mansford sensed) of inhabitants both awake and asleep, poisoning them with trouble and doubt.

The best Mansford could do was focus on but one...the dwarfish specimen that had acknowledged him with its unsettled glance.

The thing scampered through the side streets until it came upon a small, white-shingled row house, and out of sheer weariness, readapted his thick, rubbery hide, tossing the chunk of cardboard to the side, then flopped up the steps, past the threshold.

Mansford noticed that the door was, in fact, pounded and trampled. Along the threshold's fringe, the sides were fractured and splintered, as if something large had forced its way through.

Mansford followed the creature's fervid panting, and it looked back in disdain as it scampered.

Mansford stayed atop it, rushing through the doleful living room. He noticed the crushed couch, the pictures cocked on the flower-printed walls or scattered across the floor, among snapped frames and broken glass.

The beast entered the kitchen, as Mansford kicked a broken frame with his heel, noticing it was a family portrait.

He absorbed its details. Much to his surprise, the bearded man was featured, poised proud and stately in suit and tie and alongside him a fashionably dressed, middle-age woman with graying hair and between these two, only a few years younger than she was now, the golden-haired Standish.

An eerie glow fell upon the man and woman, but left the girl unstained. This had to be more than a mere coincidence. Was he being played a fool, or had fate intervened, courtesy of the creature? And if this man was, in fact, her father, how could he dare sacrifice his daughter to such a vile thing?

The dwarfish creature clawed about the kitchen, prompting Mansford to abandon the photo, and he followed, witnessing the confused beast burrowing at the back door.

Sensing his presence, the creature stopped, his expression wrought with rage.

Mansford realized, as his pearly persona entered each of its teary orbs, he was absorbing the beast's life: how it was stomped and smothered by bigger specimens, wondering if the next blow might be the one to do it in.

With a croaking hiss, the creature warned Mansford to back away, but Mansford edged closer, forcing the beast to press its back hard against the door. It sniveled, raised its arms, concealing it face, in what seemed an ill-fated attempt to shield its thoughts from Mansford's mind.

It trembled a few more seconds, then in one, fast sooty burst, disassembled, its molecules seeping into the door and upon floor, leaving a faint, shadowy impression, which then evaporated.

Saddened by the creature's unique departure, Mansford spun around, perceptive to notice the unopened mail strewn upon the counter. He moved toward it, leafed through the various bills and miscellaneous fodder, until he discerned the primary addressees: Mister Jon Pickwick and Ms. Marjorie Standish.

"Hmmm," Mansford ruminated, "Standish...Interesting she kept her maiden name, or perhaps the two are living unmarried. Either way, the better part of wisdom tells me, this fellow is unlikely the girl's biological father."

With this curious deduction, he passed back through the living room, giving it another once-over, then hovered beyond the threshold, pausing upon the front steps to sniff out his next move, when from the side, the chunk of cardboard caught his eye.

A gentle gust lifted it, revealing its claw-tipped script: BEN GYLER FOR MAYOR...A COMMON MAN FOR COMMON PEOPLE.

How basic, Mansford thought, how quaint. These creatures were, indeed, a most conniving bunch. Not only could they fashion, for whatever odd reason, a political declaration, but possessed the power to perish in a snap, but what if the latter was not so much an escape stunt, but rather a transformational stunt? Why this notion entered Mansford's head, he could not say, but for whatever reason, it made sense. Additionally, had the little monster made its way to Pickwick's abode because it believed he might still be there, maybe even the behemoth? The great beast had been there, after all. The signs were most evident.

As Mansford contemplated these diabolical possibilities, he soared onward, the streaming streetlights guiding him back from where he had traveled and before very long, he found himself soaring from out the park, landing before his building.

He entered, passing Charlie, who was immersed in a movie magazine, his feet up on the desk. Mansford then headed into the elevator, his sense of humanity resuming.

Once inside his apartment, he steadied himself and removed the mask, returning it to the drawer, his skin no longer tingling, but his mind yet ripe with thought.

He strolled to the bedroom and watched his lady roll onto her side, breathing at ease, without a hint of care.

For present sake, her complacency was good enough. Let her sleep, he thought. Tomorrow he would question her further and when the time was right, perhaps reveal the unpalatable truth about her father.

He sauntered to the couch and crawled into it, his gaze fixed on the desk drawer, drawing from it a flow of ethereal vibes. He had not felt so at peace in years, and within this assured contentment, succumbed to a well deserved sleep.

(VIII)

The alarm rang.

Mansford leapt from the couch.

"Stacey," he called, heading for the bedroom. "Stacey, my dear...you awake?"

He peered inside, saw the bed made, the closet door open, a batch of Penelope's stay-over dresses hanging from the hangers, her various shoes strewn about the floor. In the small garbage pale near the end table, a clumped night gown protruded.

"Damn," Mansford groaned. "She's flown the coup and without even a good-bye."

Flustered, he washed up, donned a fresh suit and tie, intent on tracking the young lady down, but not before pausing at the desk.

He took out the mask and strapped it onto his arm, leaving it face-down at his elbow. He grabbed an old, black silk scarf and tucked it along the mask's inner edge, concealing it.

He then headed out and met up with Charlie, who was on the verge of leaving, though quite inclined to converse.

"Hey there, Mister Mansford," he chirped as they passed the front doors. "Was wondering when you might depart. Noticed the young lady leave about a half hour ago." He snickered. "Between you and me, I believe she may have been wearing one of Ms. James' dresses."

"Oh," Mansford said. "Well, under the circumstances, I guess it's only expected. I'll look into it, though, my friend." He smiled, sprinting onward. "See you tonight."

He leapt into his Packard, zooming onto the road, scoping every direction.

● ● ●

Mansford discerned Standish's fair hair and the way the dark dress draped her slender form.

She stood on the steps of her parents' home, talking to a neighbor: a middle-age woman in a frizzy, pink robe with curlers in her hair, her pudgy upper body extending beyond the screen door.

Mansford parked a few spots down and crept his way over.

"Like I said, dear," the woman explained, "I heard some scuffing, some scraping, all fairly fast, but I was half asleep at the time. Believe it or not, I assumed it was a couple stray cats. You know how cats like to fight." She paused. "I do recall some croaking, oddly enough, like a big frog might do, then some chatting, but I'm sure I just imagined those parts. Like I said, I was half asleep, dear."

"Yes, but," Standish argued, "the damage is quite extensive. I can't help but assume someone got hurt." She looked about. "Perhaps someone else knows where my parents are."

The woman shrugged. "I'm really not sure, dear. If you'd like, though, I'd be happy to phone the police."

"Oh, would you?" Standish asked. "I'd appreciate it immensely, Mrs. Curbishley."

"All right, dear," the woman said with a nod. "I'll call right now."

The woman headed inside, while Standish teetered, her back toward Mansford, giving him ample chance to sneak up and tap her shoulder.

She spun around and upon realizing who it was, rolled her eyes to the side.

"Oh, it's you."

"Indeed, it is, Ms. Harlow," he jested. "May I be so bold to ask for an autograph?"

"I'm sorry, Mike," she muttered, avoiding the joke. "I didn't want to wake you. I figured you wouldn't mind if I borrowed Miss James' clothes. I thought it best I get home before…"

"Your father scolded you?"

She rolled her eyes again and fighting back the tears said, "Yes, more or less." She then glanced at the damaged doorway. "It'll probably be chalked up as a basic break-in, but we both know otherwise…don't we?"

"Well," Mansford said, "a break-in's a break-in, no matter what the actual cause," but then tested the waters by asking, "Nonetheless, did you, by chance, look inside? Anything taken?"

"Yes, I looked," she said. "Nothing was taken that I could detect." Her expression then turned suspicious. "Say, how did you know where I live?"

"It wasn't hard," Mansford ad-libbed. "I looked you up in the phone book, under your name."

"But the phone book lists only my step-father…Pickwick."

"I have a special directory," he continued, "for business purposes, you see…cross references all to a tee."

"I see," she said. "Well, I guess it's just as well you found me. My neighbor, Mrs. Curbishley, is calling the police. It's probably just as well you're here. You were supposed to go back to the cemetery to converse with them, weren't you?"

"Yes," said Mansford. "I ended up talking to Jack Murphy, the local beat cop. He actually met up with me at the penthouse, then we drove to Blessed Tidings. He took note of the situation, but in all honesty, there wasn't much I could convincingly convey, since when we arrived, everything appeared back to normal; not a solitary trace of any damage. Even Fred and Pete appeared unscathed and to worsen matters, claimed I had been drinking. Nice…"

"That makes no sense," she charged. "There's simply no way…"

"Ah," Mansford interrupted, "there's far more to this than meets the eye, and I fear certain participants may be more closely connected than we dared realize."

"Meaning?" she asked with a dash of further suspicion.

"I'm talking something evil here; forces that can create the illusion of stability when there's none." He pointed to the house. "I'm surprised this wasn't covered up as well, but then the remnants of such are probably of little consequence, compared to the cemetery." He glared at her, hard and unflinching. "I'll come clean with you, Stacey. By hook or by crook, I found my way here last night. I also know your father is involved in all this. He was among the cultists gathered at the cemetery; the apparent leader, in fact. He undoubtedly had you drugged, then he and his crony grabbed you, and the fact that you can't place their faces or associate their names could simply be a result of your inebriation, but then, your subconscious mind could also be denying you the truth. This is, after all, quite a hefty form of betrayal."

"I'm sorry, but I can't believe that," she said and started to sob. "This is so terribly confusing. Really, I'm not trying to hide anything, deny anything. I'm sorry if you don't believe me."

He felt bad for upsetting her. "It's not that at all," he said, recalling her innocent glow from the night before. "Like you, I'm just trying to understand." He reached out, tempted to pull her close, and restrained himself. "That's all, Stacy."

Curbishley reappeared, though hesitated when she spotted Mansford.

"Oh, uh, Stacey, dear, I called the station. They'll send someone over as soon as they can." She shot Mansford a wary glance. "You're not by chance from the police, are you?"

"No," Mansford replied. "Just a friend."

The woman's stance softened. "I see," she said, squinting. "I must say, you do look quite familiar. Perhaps I've seen you around."

"I'd imagine," said Mansford. "After all, I do generally make the rounds."

The woman smiled, patted her curlers and in an evident state of embarrassment, slinked back inside.

When he was confident she was beyond earshot, he continued, "At this point, I doubt the police will be of much help. Perhaps if we go somewhere, collect our thoughts; we can unravel this in our own way, on our own time."

Standish nodded, letting Mansford take her hand, but as he led her, her oversized shoes slipped off.

"For heaven's sake," she mumbled, noticing one had landed near a piece of cardboard. "Would you look at that?" She put on the shoes, reached down and handed the scrap to Mansford. "How silly. Everyone knows Mayor Poindexter is running uncontested."

The mask emitted sharp signals into Mansford's elbow, the vibrations riding up into his arm, then his head. His eyes sparked with revelation.

"Let's hold onto this, okay?" he said.

"Sure, but why?"

"Consider it a little proof-in-the-pudding," he explained. "We're going to pay a visit to the Brink Town Times." He grabbed her arm, pulled fast. "If anyone would know of a potential campaign challenge, as well as any number of other brewing shenanigans, it would be the editor-in-chief, and he just happens to be a friend of mine…"

(IX)

"Course, I don't mind," said Carl Clive. "Come in, Mike. You and the young lady are more than welcome. Make yourselves comfortable."

Clive was a shrewd, white-haired gent in his early seventies. In the annals of the Brink Town Times, he had done right by the Mansford name, and when it came to any socialite updates, ensured his reporters were tactful, particularly when it came to Miss James.

"So, young lady," he said, scrutinizing Standish's comely face, "are you one of Ms. James' nieces? You rather do dress like her, I must say. Yeah, fashion certainly does run in the family, doesn't it?"

"I'm sorry," Standish explained, "but I'm not related." She squeezed around the piles of old newspapers and assorted office supplies to reach her chair. "You might say, in this instance, I'm just along for the ride."

"I see," said Clive, his eyes shifting to Mansford. "I see, indeed. So, you two are here on a mission, I take it, after an inside scoop, perhaps?"

Mansford took a seat alongside her, locked his fingers and regarded Clive from across the desk. "Hoping to confirm something via the grapevine, Carl." He then presented the cardboard. "This little diddy resonate?"

Clive scanned it and chuckled, "Nice calligraphy, but obviously a gag." He looked at it again. "Gyler…Gyler…I'll admit, though, the name does sound familiar, but for the life of me, I can't say." He returned the cardboard to Mansford and rapped his fingers along the edge of his desk. His eyes widened. "Gosh, but of course. How could I be so forgetful?" He lifted a small slither of paper from the side. "My secretary got a call this morning to place a full-page ad. I just didn't have time to read it, let alone associate it with a mayoral challenge. Full-page ads are expensive, you know. We rarely get such requests from just anybody."

"So, what's the deal?" Mansford asked.

"Well," said Clive, "it's a political ad, all right, basically calls Poindexter a pawn of the rich and to vote for Ben Gyler, Champion of the Common Folk." He shook his head and handed the slither to Mansford. "Guess it clicks, but what a contrast, from a crummy piece of cardboard to such a costly spread."

Mansford scrutinized the request, handed it back. "Doesn't say who placed it."

"My secretary did mention the name." Clive snapped his fingers. "Yes, it was the MCC...whatever the hell that stands for. My people will check it. The last thing we want is some group with a radical agenda. From a business perspective, such could backfire."

"I suspect," said Mansford, "this particular group might just fall into that category, and Ben Gyler, if that's really his name, is the culprit helming it."

"Pretty strong words, Mike." He then looked to Standish. "So, what do you know about this Gyler guy?"

"Not a lot at this point," Mansford confessed, pulling Clive's attention back to him, "but I, for one, have reason to believe he's up to no good. I've also a hunch a batch of these homespun signs will end up about town, with a professional ad just adding more fuel to the fire. Heck, it's only July, so who knows? By the time November hits, perhaps Poindexter might have a viable opponent on his hands."

"Anything's possible," said Clive, "but I wouldn't bet on this joker. If he really wants to make a serious bid, it's going to take more than cardboard signs and a big-priced ad to drive home his point. His supporters will have to establish their headquarters smack in the heart of Brink Town, network like crazy to get the word out, and to be truly effective, do it like now. Trust me, Mike, it's a lot harder than it sounds."

Mansford glanced at Standish, who pulled the cardboard from him, stared at it and sighed.

"I appreciate your insight," Mansford said, reaching for Clive's hand as he stood. "At least we know this is at best a pipe dream."

"No problem," said Clive, giving Mansford a firm shake. "You're always welcome here, Mike." He gave Standish a wink as he rose, "You, too, young lady." He smiled. "You sure you're not related to Miss James?"

"I'm quite sure," she iterated, tucking the cardboard under her arm as she moved with a dissatisfied pout toward Mansford.

"Oh, well," said Clive, "no big deal one way or the other, I suppose." He gave Mansford a cautious glance and whispered from the side of his mouth, "You say hello to Penelope, will you? Tell her I hope she's doing well."

"Of course," said Mansford. "I'll be sure to do that, Carl."

The couple then hobbled through the stacks, side-stepping their way to the door.

"Oh, Mike, just one more thing."

"Yeah, Carl."

"I may not know what the deal is with this Gyler character, if he even has an inkling of political clout, but if he really does start to mount any momentum, throw your full weight behind Poindexter. Poor ol' Percy may not be the most dynamic politician, but at least he's honest. He'll need whatever help he can get if he's going up against anyone who's otherwise."

Mansford smiled and nodded. "Sounds like sound advice to me," he said. "We'll converse later, my friend..."

As he and Standish cut through the buzzing bodies and clicking typewriters, he said, "The campaign offices always set up on Main Street. One faction almost always occupies the old, general store, rotating with the Christmas-tree vendors and income-tax assessors, depending on the time of year."

"Yes, but," Standish asked, "what are the chances of that?"

"My hunch is high," said Mansford, grazing the mask, his mental gears cranking fast. "In fact, a little voice tells me, we need only go directly to the source."

(X)

The morning traffic proved irritating, taking apparent forever to get to Main Street, and the store front was still a good stretch away. Mansford rather wished he could don the mask, float his way there, but this was neither the time nor the place for such celestial conveniences.

Meanwhile, as they waited at the light, Standish began to fidget.

"I appreciate what you're doing," she said, "but there's a more pressing concern, namely my parents. I figured that going to the newspaper wouldn't reveal anything substantial, but was at least willing to entertain the prospect. I fear we'll never get back on track. Perhaps you should take me home, or better yet, let's go straight to the police station, and avoid any further dead ends."

"We'll still have to pass the store to get there," Mansford explained, "so just relax. Can't hurt to have a glance as we drive by."

Mansford felt ebbing warmth engulf his arm, as if the mask were in some way egging him on.

He glanced at Standish, savoring her Harlow-esque features, contemplating her age, her good standing in this dire situation, and though one part of him insisted he harden his heart, another part could not help but be drawn to her. In fact, he could not help but think they shared an indivisible connection. How strange, considering the short time since they had met.

"I want you to know," he said, "you're more than welcome to stay with me throughout all this. The worst thing you could do is wing it alone."

She avoided his gaze and said, "Once I get some satisfactory answers, I'll decide what to do."

He dismissed her aloofness and was glad when the traffic light changed.

Within a very short distance, Main Street appeared, prompting Mansford to exclaim, "Yes, that's the building up ahead." He discerned a group of people milling about the store front. "Hmmm...Why am I not surprised?"

"What is it?" Standish asked, leaning forward to see, as a couple men crossed the street, hoisting cardboard, stick-strapped signs. "Oh, yes, I see."

"Yep," Mansford confirmed, "they moved like lightning on this." He pulled into a spot across the street from the store. "Let's have a look, shall we?"

With a sigh, Standish agreed, and as they waited for the traffic to pass, they caught a glimpse at what transpired behind the store window: desks dragged, telephones slapped atop them, and in the backdrop, posters tacked, but not the vagabond kind. These were large, clean with white, bright backgrounds and fresh blue and red print: GYLER FOR MAYOR... HAIL THE COMMON MAN.

"The utter audacity," Mansford grumbled, grabbing her hand and leading her onward. "To use the stately pigments of Old Glory to conceal their evil...simply blasphemous."

"I'm not sure what you mean," Standish said.

"Swastikas would suit them better," Mansford explained, swinging her over the curb, "or perhaps the overlap of a hammer and sickle...any of those modern insignia to convey all things suppressive, but then it's the habit of bad people to hide behind lies."

They stepped onto the pavement and headed toward the door, when quite unexpected, a familiar bearded man exited, looking confident and smart in his three-piece suit and diamond-clipped tie, at least until his daughter caught his eye.

Mansford's initial reaction was to slug him, but before he could raise his fist, the man exclaimed, "Stacey…how splendid. So…so, there you are. I'm so happy to see you're fine."

"Likely story," she shrieked and darted behind Mansford, allowing a series of brisk images to enter his head: her father hovering near her bed, over his henchman's shoulder, the chloroform cloth settling under her nose, her limp limbs lifted, carted toward the family car…

Pickwick, meanwhile, sized Mansford up and with tremulous contempt, declared, "My, my, it's you; the meddling graveyard hero." He cocked his head, absorbing the rest of Mansford's frame. "Yes, you changed after you ascended and threw our sacrificial plan asunder." He laughed. "You even went back to the scene later that night; or so a vision told me. You saw through our idyllic veil. The demons whispered it to me. They said you floated on the air, chased them all away." He then spun around, opened the door and screamed inside, "Carmine…hurry, quick. The enemy's in our midst."

A dashingly attired Pascale jaunted from the rear, while Pickwick grabbed Mansford's arm, his fingers grazing his elbow and with it, the mask.

"Owwww," Pickwick groaned, springing back, wringing his wrist. "You self-righteous clod…you've…you've burnt me."

Pascale paused, began to step back, as those inside maneuvered around.

Mansford's body vibrated and up shot his arm.

Everyone gasped.

Like a spotlight, the pearl face beamed through its silk concealment, growing ever brighter, to the point where Pascale raised his hands to block the rays, with others following suit.

Anguished moans and wails burst about the chamber, while Pickwick teetered on the outskirts, bouncing onto the sidewalk, whimpering and seething, "You may think you've gained leverage, but nothing you can do will uproot our plans."

Mansford stepped backward and again took Standish's hand, as she craned her neck to see what had transpired.

He did not give her much time to analyze, whispering, "We may have been a trifle hasty to come here, but at least we've given them a good fright. Now, watch your step, my dear. We're getting out of here."

They turned and zigzagged across the street, through the traffic, boarding the Packard just as Pickwick skidded off the curb.

Mansford revved the engine and roared past him, tapping his elbow in threat. Then from his rearview mirror, he watched the corrupt sophisticate leaping about, until he became little more than a flailing speck.

(XI)

"Oh, this is just horrid," Standish whined, as Mansford rolled onto the highway. "You were so right, Mike. And to think it's been my own father, no less. I guess I was in denial. I guess I couldn't accept the truth; that no-good bastard."

"Well, you more than implied he wasn't a nice guy," said Mansford. "This just puts an extra layer on that particular cake."

"And mother?" Standish asked. "She wasn't with him. Maybe he…oh, no, he couldn't have." She trembled. "We really do need the police, Mike. This is far worse than either of us imagined."

Mansford sighed. "I'm still hesitant about that, Stacey. After all, your father is right about one thing. Whatever this plot entails, it's taken serious root. I mean, for all we know, it could very well extend to the police." He gave her a sorrowful glance. "Tell me, Stacey, when your father's not indulging in monster conjuring, what does he do…what sort of work?"

"He's the curator at the Brink Town Museum," she said. "He specializes in ancient history. You'd be surprised by the curious things he comes across." She considered her words. "Why do you ask?"

"And how about this other guy," Mansford asked, "this Carmine gent?"

"Carmine Pascale, you mean," she answered, the name flowing venomously from her lips, rubbing her nose in remembrance of the chloroform. "He's head honcho at the Brink Town Library. For what it's worth, my mother works there, in the reference section. Carmine got her the job: a favor to my father. That's also how I got a part-time position. He's never given any indication of being anything but helpful."

Mansford frowned. "I'm starting to see how one thing connects to the other. And these jobs, by their very nature, are relegated to public view. Folks would know who works where; seek help from these individuals on occasion. Some, perhaps, might even hold connections of their own, even help pull a few strings to get certain things done, if they were disgruntled enough to join some potentially prestigious cult."

"You really believe people would do that?" Standish asked.

"Honestly, Stacey, it's as likely a prospect as any. Nonetheless, it's best we be careful, stick to only those we know, and even then, be very cautious. At this point, I don't know what guise the Great Beguiler may have adapted, but if he's truly Ben Gyler, he's undoubtedly using another form. In fact, my instincts tell me his current façade is probably unassuming…maybe even trustworthy."

They traveled a tad further, then exited onto a ramp, which led to a quaint, tree-queued pass.

"So, now where?" she asked.

"My favorite place of business," he said. "There's someone I need to converse with, someone skilled at getting things done. I think you'll like him, actually. His name's Ned…Ned Stark."

●●●

They pulled up to the large, gray-brick building. The humongous, steel sign atop it featured a pointy-capped, frilly-collared clown, his head angled, his painted lips wide with laugher and beneath him, in flamboyant P.T. Barnum scroll: ESOTERIC INCORPORATED…NOVELTIES ARE OUR GAME, est 1892.

As if expecting their arrival, Stark popped from out the front door and ambled over.

"Saw you heading in from the workshop window," he said, as Mansford stepped from his car and Standish from the other side. "I was hoping you might be here earlier. I got that paperwork all set to sign. We'll have those rubber hands in production in less than a month." He glanced at Standish, who offered a smile. "Say there, who's your pretty friend?"

"Her name's Stacey Standish," Mansford replied, hoping to avoid small talk. "She's assisting me on an assignment. I was hoping you might possibly help as well, Ned."

"Assignment?" Stark said. "Assignments are my creed. Tell me what you need."

"For one," Mansford answered, "our annual Gag Festival pushed up a month."

"For heaven sakes, why?" Stark asked, as Mansford and Standish followed him toward the entrance. "You know how hard they are to arrange, particularly with the mayor's schedule as it is…unless of course, you want a different master of ceremonies. Percy would be heart-broken, though."

"Mayor Poindexter must attend," Mansford insisted, "and because he's so sentimental of our shindigs, I'm sure he'll happily subscribe to the rescheduling. I also want the press in attendance. I'm sure Carl will oblige on that, but you make a few follow-up calls to him, to coax things along.

"You really believe people would do that?"

Oh, and just to be on the safe side, we'll need a bigger banquet hall: one that holds at least twice as many as we've catered before."

Stark sighed. "And what meal do you wished served this year?"

"Doesn't matter, as long as there's plenty of ice cream and cake in the wake."

"Come clean, Mike," said Stark, shooting Standish a playful wink as he held open the door. "What devilish plan do you have up your sleeve?"

Mansford laughed. "Trust me, Ned, there's nothing devilish about it, at least not on my end."

"Ice-cream and cake," Stark mumbled, following them into the hall, its walls clustered with framed posters of fairs and circuses. "Wait a minute. I sure as hell hope you're not going to ask those rowdy orphans to attend. We're still paying for the damage those rascals caused back in thirty-three."

"Trust me," Mansford said. "Despite the probable consequences, their presence is essential. Contact Brink Town Transit. The kids can be transported by bus. Father Bruno can supply you the precise number."

Stark grumbled under his breath, but donned a pretentious smile as he escorted them to his work shop, which Standish soon realized, far exceeded even Clive's haphazard mess.

In this regard, though Mansford and Stark knew right where to meander, she tripped her way between towers of confetti-brimmed boxes, around tables lumped with headless ventriloquist dummies, disassembled joy buzzers and stacks of whoopee cushions. She was also blinded by the smoky sunlight that filtered its way in and was grateful when they reached the rear work bench, where a batch of fake hands were piled, as well as the evident paperwork at its center.

"Here you go," said Stark, pushing the sheets toward Mansford, along with a pen. "It's the last four pages you need to sign."

Mansford obliged, while Stark gave Standish another curious scan, forcing her to glance away.

"And there you go," said Mansford, pushing the items back to him. "It's too bad we can't get the bulk of the Creepy Crawling Hands produced sooner."

"Well, the prototypes will at least convey what's on the horizon," said Stark. "The mayor can even sport one when he steps out on stage…a guaranteed hoot and a half."

"No doubt," Mansford said and stepped toward a stack of dusty boxes along the far wall, their big, stamped labels declaring: RUBBER FRIGHT RATS.

"Oh, yeah," said Stark, "those sold under expectations, but I always thought they were kinda nifty." He scooted over to Mansford, reached into the top box and pulled out a plump rodent, its eyes wide, its saber-toothed incisors protruding. He then placed it against his chest, squeezed its body hard, forcing its mouth to open, so that it emitted a long, shrill squeak. "Clever, don't you think?"

Mansford drummed his cheek. "How many would you say we have?"

"Hundreds," Stark admitted, tossing the rat back into the box. "Unfortunately, one never knows what'll catch on."

"As I recall, Ned, we had a problem with the distribution company on those. Given another chance, another venue for promotional purposes, who can say?"

Stark winced. "You're not thinking what I think you're thinking, are you?"

Mansford smirked. "Indeed, you are, Ned, but one additional thing. I'd like little, paper collars around their necks, each printed with the same name."

Stark shrugged. "I guess I could work that. What name, Mike?"

"Ben Gyler," Mansford said and even spelt it out.

"Gotcha," said Stark, jotting it onto the back of his hand. "Consider it done. Anything else?"

"Yes," said Mansford. "If you can, I'd like you to investigate a few people for me."

"Detective work, you mean?"

"Indeed," said Mansford, placing a consoling hand upon Standish's shoulder, as if to brace her for what he was about to say. "The names are Jon Pickwick...no "h" in Jon, by the way...Marjorie Standish...Carmine Pascale. The first works for the museum, the latter two for the library. Got that, Ned?"

"Loud and clear," he said, jotting those also onto his hand.

Standish, meanwhile, squirmed from out Mansford's grasp and sputtered, "My mother certainly wouldn't be involved in anything so unsavory, and as for our sharing the same last name, how would you know, Mike, or is it that special directory you told me about?"

"Let's just say," Mansford explained, "last night's events blessed me with a few advanced tidbits, and as for Ned's research, it might actually reveal where your mother is, and a lot faster than if we went through the so-called proper channels. Ned can find out whether she's okay or in harm's way, and from there, we can intercede accordingly."

"I'm sorry, Mike," she said, "but I won't stand for it." She folded her arms over her chest. "I don't mind the matter being investigated via the police, or even a hired professional, but I'm sorry, I won't settle for it being done through some whimsical, inside-man, with all due respects to Mister Stark."

Mansford pouted, wondering how he might get around the matter, when a speck of revelation entered his head: one that he could not quite yet discern, but which he still decided to invest his faith.

"Very well, Stacey," he said. "I'll abide by your wishes." He shrugged at Stark, who then motioned to rub the names away. "Any investigating will be done through police authority only, and if you give me more time, I'll personally initiate it."

He then turned from her and with utmost conviction informed Stark, "I've only one more request, and despite it being even more toward the arcane, it's a must." He tugged the silk from his elbow and tossed it on the table and removed the mask. "For when I'm not actually wearing it, I'll need something to conceal it, cushion it, if you will." He set the mask on the table, allowing the sunlight to dance off its pearly surface. "It's got to be light, Ned, and designed in such a way as not to cause it any damage... that is, if it can, in fact, be damaged. There's so much I've yet to learn about it, you see."

As the sunlight continued to beam, the mask churned rings of golden light, which lingered but for a few seconds, before disappearing, with another round following.

"Mesmerizing," said Stark. "Where did you get it?"

Standish cleared her throat. "He came out of the ground with it," she said, her tone drawled as she absorbed the lovely phenomenon. "I was at the cemetery last night, when he saved me." She regarded Mansford. "You never did say how you attained it, though, did you?"

"Sounds like quite a tale," Stark interjected, his eyes still transfixed. "What does she mean...you, uh, came out of the ground?"

"I fell in when I was trying to rescue her from this colossal beast," he replied, the need for words feeling obsolete, and in their place and from the billowing rays, sound-tinged images beamed for them to see: hooded folks scampering about, the ground quaking, cracking; something big and black emerging, Mansford falling down; an orange glow ebbing upward, drawing him ever deeper down into it; a smoky-faced man beckoning, then handing the baffled Mansford the shimmering, nondescript face.

They heard Surrogate's words, but not in the traditional sense, for their implied meaning wove throughout their minds like thread sewing cloth. Their faces tingled, their bodies felt light, and when they envisioned themselves returning to the surface, the behemoth reared, but as they looked upon it…with hard, impenetrable concentration…it quivered and fled.

"Whoa," Stark gasped, shaking his head, sweat flowing from his brow. "What the hell was that?"

Standish shook and grabbed Mansford's hand, but he remained stoic and stiff, his eyes still fixed on the mask, even though the glow had faded.

"Mike," Standish pleaded, "snap out of it. Mike…please."

Stark reached over and nudged him. "Yeah, come on, Mike, wake up, will yah?"

Mansford blinked, stepped back and muttered, "My God, what an invigorating thing to relive." He then smiled, moved closer to the table, his fingers falling upon the mask, tracing it. "You see what I mean? There's so much yet to learn, so much yet to do." He inhaled lovingly, exhaled determinately. "Somehow, someway, this mask will show me the truth…in fact, show anyone who dares believe in it and respects its power."

"Well, I, for one, have no problem believing," said Stark, leaning over to better ascertain the object's shape and scope. "I think I can help you, Mike, and in that, I sense time is of the essence, I'll whip up something by tonight. I'll keep it light and thin, but at the same time, sturdy and strong." He held up Mansford's arm, patting his friend's side, checking the distance between his lower arm and upper hip. "Indeed, I do believe I've something that can work."

"Thanks," said Mansford. "The positioning is most important: a nice, inconspicuous place that doesn't get in the way." He turned to Standish and said, "We really should go. We've another stop to make."

"Terrific," said Standish, sounding less than pleased.

He then reattached the mask to his elbow and the silk around it.

"So long, Ned," he said with an assured flash of his forearm. "We'll touch base later."

"Sure," said Stark, still starry-eyed, "one way or the other, my friend. You be careful now. You hear?" He pointed to Standish. "That goes for you, too, Miss."

"Don't worry," said Mansford, as he led her through the maze. "We've got this thing under control."

They then shot from the building and in a snap, were back on the highway.

(XII)

"**I**s it really necessary we return to the cemetery?" Standish asked. "You've already told me these *things*...whatever they are...created some kind of cloaking device. Doesn't that suffice? Why risk provoking the situation?"

"At this point," Mansford countered, "I'm still not a hundred-percent certain what's transpired, or if even what I had encountered still stands. I want to look around, get a further handle on things. If I sense any danger, I've got the mask. Don't worry, we'll be fine."

"What of those groundskeepers? You said they were hypnotized or something, right? What if they're lurking? I mean, at the very least, can't we just peek in through the fence?"

Mansford made a sharp turn, and much to Standish's lament, the cemetery came into view.

"Why look there," he said. "The front gates are open."

"That can't be a good sign," she replied. "The gates are generally locked at this time, aren't they? That means someone opened them. Someone...or something...is undoubtedly inside. That spells trouble."

Mansford could not deny the peculiarity, but decided it best not to feed into Standish's fear, though the explanation became clear as they neared the work house.

"Hey, that's Phil Sutton," Mansford said, pointing to an older man sauntering in the near distance, his back turned to them. "He must have opened early. He often does that to get away from his wife."

Mansford beeped his horn, making Sutton turn.

He was dressed in jeans and a flannel shirt: further indication he was there on his day off. His expression, however, looked grim, and to substantiate it, Officer Murphy then appeared from the side, still dressed casually, his expression as dour.

"Who's that other man?" asked Standish.

"Jack Murphy," said Mansford, "the officer who accompanied me here last night when everything looked, as it does now, nice and smoothed over." He parked the car, turned off the engine, taking a moment to tap the wheel. "Wonder what brought Murphy back, especially if he's off duty. Anyway, my dear, his presence may help kick off your authoritative search."

Sutton approached as the two exited. "Hey, there, Mike," he said, then nodded at Standish, though his interest in her appeared at best minimal. "Good timing. I was just about to call you."

"So I'd assume," said Mansford, his gaze falling upon the steely-eyed Murphy. "Am I out of line to presume there's a new development?"

"Right you are," Sutton quipped, "and from what the officer tells me, it happened last night. I just picked up some of the remnants." He pointed to the side of the house, where several unfinished posters and paint cans were stacked. "You should have called me, Mike. I'd have appreciated the update."

"Sorry about that, Phil. Figured I'd give you the scoop when you returned."

He smirked. "Well, you know how I like to visit during off hours. Besides, Fred and Pete called me earlier, claimed they have the flu or some such thing. Didn't mention a damn thing about last night, but I'd expect that from those knuckleheads." He cocked his thumb toward Murphy. "The officer says it was delinquents this time, but I stand by what I saw the night before. How 'bout you, Mike? What's your take?"

"Delinquents," Mansford lied, recalling the youngsters he had deposited at the station. "As Officer Murphy implied, there's a growing problem..."

"Listen," said Murphy, detecting the edge to Mansford's voice. "It's swell if you and Mister Sutton have different angles on this. I'd also like to apologize for being hasty with you gents. I should know, after all, there's often more to a crime scene than meets the eye." He kicked the grass. "This could be such a case in point."

"We appreciate the change of heart," said Mansford.

"Well, it's no big revelation on my part," said Murphy, pointing to the posters. "For one thing, I've seen this guy's name plastered all over town, like it's some sort of overnight epidemic...but in a cemetery? Nah, that's just taking it too far. It feels bad."

"So," Standish said, "even with that, you still maintain it's children?"

Murphy laughed, signaling his delinquent concept was at best a pretext. "I can't say who's doing what actually. I only know something's off-kilter, based on what I've accumulated." His eyes shifted to Sutton, then back to Mansford. "Okay, I'll come clean. Two kids ended up at the station last night, just as I was leaving. They were a bit hysterical to say the least. They mentioned being accosted by some sort of specter." He pointed to his face. "They said his head was as white as a ghost and all aglow, if you can believe that."

"And of course," said Mansford, "you don't believe that."

"I must say, the little bastards seemed sincere," Murphy affirmed. "Hell, they found the whole excursion unnerving enough to confess to a long line of petty crimes. Of course, whoever they saw was in disguise. You fellows did say, after all, there were folks here dressed like monks. Maybe it was one of them on his way home, figured he'd give the kids a nice scare with a glow-in-the-dark false face…probably one from your very own novelty shop, Mister Mansford. Also, that they claim this character actually carried them through the air…well, heck, hysterics can generally throw off one's perception." He shook his head. "Who knows? Maybe that'll be this new candidate's pledge. These oddballs stage a few crazy events, stir up some delinquents, and then claim they've got themselves someone who can clean up the streets. Nice slap in the face to the police, though, that would be."

"I see," said Mansford. "What do your fellow boys in blue think?"

"Oh, this is just speculation on my end," Murphy said. "I took care of the youngsters myself, made out the entire report. The captain was nice enough to grant me overtime, since we were a tad short. I'm assuming the folks down at Juvenile Hall will now tend to the matter. For now, that's pretty much it."

Mansford absorbed the officer's aura, his sense of duty, his tenacity to see things through. Yes, Murphy knew something was awry, even if he could not precisely identify it.

"If you'd excuse me, officer…" said Mansford, ushering Standish off to the side.

Standish assumed the worse and whispered, "He's lying, right?"

"No, I believe he's sincere," Mansford said, "and wants to help." Mansford looked back at Murphy, their eyes again meeting, the bond of trust forming. "As a police officer, he can get us into places we wouldn't have access to. He can even look into the situation with your parents. At any rate, my instincts tell me this is the way to go. If you think about it, it's still basically what you want, of course."

Standish bit her lip, shook her head no, but the worry in her eyes said otherwise.

Mansford turned from her and approached the officer. "Would you be willing to help me check on a few people who might be involved with this, officer?"

"In what capacity?" Murphy asked.

"Well, at this point, it's more a matter of merely checking their primary stomping grounds: that is, their places of employment. You see, it might prove a bit disconcerting if I were to show up where they work, started poking around, and with you being an officer of the law and all…"

Murphy winced. "I never overstep my bounds," he said, "on or off duty." He paused, though, and looked back at the posters. "However, if you think it might help…"

"Yes," said Mansford, "I truly do." He smiled. "Maybe we can go together, at least to get things started."

Murphy hesitated, but then nodded.

"I'll drive you, of course," said Mansford. "Do you, uh, need a change of attire, something more officious, perhaps?"

Murphy pulled out his wallet, revealing his badge. "This'll hold enough weight if anyone should question. Nonetheless, folks around here generally know me, maybe even better than they know you, Mister Mansford."

Mansford grinned and looked to Standish. "At this point, Stacey, it's probably best you head back to the apartment." He stroked her cheek as a means to squash an argument and whispered. "It'll be better this way… safer. Phil will take you, in fact13"

Standish shook her head and stomped. "That's ever so unfair, Mike. I've played your game all morning, and for what? If your sojourn leads to information on my mother, my parents, then I should be…"

Mansford clamped her mouth, his arm vibrating, his fingers surging with a sudden, comforting impulse that numbed her face, soothed her mind. "You have to trust me on this. I can't say how I know, but, well, I just do." He removed his hand. "You can relax, lounge around. There's a stack of fashion catalogs in the magazine rack. Penny brought them. You can order whatever you want, get yourself a whole new wardrobe. They'll send out a tailor. It'll help pass the time until I get home. I'll update you on everything. I promise."

One part of her wished to protest, but try as she may, the words did not come, and so she threw up her hands and looked toward Sutton.

"Did I hear my name?" the old gent asked. "You need a ride, dear?"

"Yes," said Mansford, "she does." He then turned toward Murphy. "Hey, where did he go?"

Sutton pointed in back of him. "Toward the mausoleum, I think."

Mansford leapt after him, watching the officer cut across portions into which he should have fallen. He had no idea of how masterful the desecration had been concealed, but then in many respects, nor did Mansford.

The vibrations, however, continued to shoot through his arm, inspiring him to remove the silk, then the mask, which he poised near his face.

The veil of normality faded from view, at best a chalkish outline superimposed over the actual ramshackled landscape, and over the crevasses, Murphy continued to stroll, his feet trailing the air, switching back and forth over both indentations and solidifying, as though the extremes were indivisible.

The officer then stopped, one foot stationed upon the soil, the other poised atop the center of a hole. He glanced at Mansford, scanning him, but did not acknowledge the mask.

"This place is poisoned," Murphy said with deep affirmation. "I don't know how I failed to sense it before. Maybe it took those youngsters to trigger something in my head, and then seeing those posters this morning… well, whatever it is, it's happening fast, like lightning let loose from a bottle, striking every which way we turn." He squinted and raised his hand, as if to divert the mask's brightening sheen. "You obviously sense it, too, Mister Mansford. That goes without saying, but I guess even in his own way, Phil Sutton also does, as well as that pretty, young lady. It's in her expression… that look that tells you, something's far from right."

Mansford lowered the mask.

"Yes," said Mansford, reattaching it to his arm, "something bad is happening. I'm sure glad you sense it, officer. That's a big plus for our side."

Murphy rubbed his eyes. "There's no doubt the lines are drawn, Mister Mansford. I can't say exactly how or why, but maybe our investigative sojourn will help settle it."

"Well, come on then," said Mansford with an encouraging wave. "Let's get this show on the road."

Murphy marched toward him, while Sutton escorted Standish toward his old pick-up.

Standish looked back at Mansford as Sutton pulled off, frowning like a lost puppy in fear of losing her master, and like one who knows the benefit a beloved pet, Mansford smiled at her, assuring her all would be right.

(XIII)

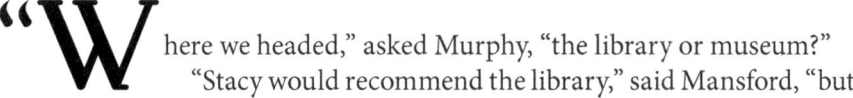

"**W**here we headed," asked Murphy, "the library or museum?"

"Stacy would recommend the library," said Mansford, "but

its unlikely her mother's there, or that anyone working today would know her whereabouts. No, we should focus first on the museum. Hands-down, Pickwick appears the catalyst. Anything even remotely linked to him will help shed light."

Murphy noticed a few more makeshift Gyler posters on the Brink Town Grocery facade and cringed. "And what's our story once we arrive, Mister Mansford?"

"Let's say I've donated a few items to the museum," he explained, "a few Aztec or Mayan pieces, and I merely wish to verify their safe arrival… to chat with Mister Pickwick on their inevitable display. You flash your badge, of course, just to show everything is being done by the book and that it's okay for us to roam about even though Pickwick isn't present. Should work, don't you think?"

"I sure hope so," Murphy groaned. "Then again, our options are slim without a warrant."

They pulled up to the museum and dashed for the building's ornate façade, noticing a Gyler sign stuck to one of its Grecian pillars, yet another alongside the fringed doorway.

"Mind-boggling," Murphy mumbled, but despite the perplexing posts, the two pressed on, Murphy's badge exposed well before they even reached the front desk.

"Hello, I'm Officer Jack Murphy," he announced to the oversized guard, who glanced up from a creased copy of the Brink Town Times. "I'm here with Mister Michael Mansford to touch base with Mister Jon Pickwick, regarding several donated artifacts."

"Donations?" the guard asked. "Mansford…you say?"

"Yes, donations," Murphy repeated, slapping his wallet shut, "from Mister Michael Mansford…surely, you've heard of him, sir."

Mansford stepped away, not out of disrespect to Murphy, but rather because halfway down the nearest aisle, three objects in a glass case had caught his eye.

Each sculpture was a different size, all black, with four, purplish jewels for eyes, four bone-clawed appendages extending from their torsos, four beneath the abdomens, their roundish husks reared in similar battle-like poses.

Mansford read the bronze-trimmed card situated before the largest:

"THE GUANER…A species of mythical monsters known to the Alamanni tribe, circa 211 AD, in the region now known as united Germany. Alleged to have been conjured by its dark-robed council members to fend off Roman rule before an unsteady alliance was formed between the factions…Despite their bestial attributes, the creatures were said to be cunning, enlightening those who worshipped them. The specimens allegedly resided in Earth's nether regions (some claim, Hades) and were distinguished by a variety of sizes, but could adapt to any terrestrial environment, assimilating like chameleons to their immediate surroundings…The encased representations are constructed of straw and animal excrement: preserved by an impermeable mixture of human blood, crushed chicken bone, dirt and an undefined herbal-based paste… Procured by Jon Pickwick, Curator, Brink Town Museum, June 1938."

Mansford's arm began to tingle, rise, the mask pushing toward the glass as if magnetized. The pearly structure thudded along the front, then toward the top, until Mansford managed to restrain it, forcing his hand down to his side.

"Easy there, fellow," he told it, glancing back at the desk, where Murphy and the guard yet conversed.

"I will absolutely not give you money to inspect the donations, sir," Murphy continued, "nor will Mister Mansford. As you are aware, I am an officer of the law."

As the two continued to spar, Mansford glanced up at the brass-braced second floor: a line of oak doors with name-plates on them. He tiptoed around the case, toward the stairs and in a flash, ascended.

His eyes passed an endless stretch of meaningless names, until the farthest one grabbed his attention: JON PICKFORD, CURATOR.

He looked about and then turned the knob, but of course, it would not budge, at least not until the vibrations refueled his fingers, warming the metal, popping the lock.

He reached inside, clicked on the light and was stunned by what he saw.

Beyond the predictable inclusion of chairs and a wide, drape-drawn window, a long table centered the chamber, atop which were tripod-propped vials of strange herbs and spices, crystal pitchers of foul-scented liquids that ranged from devilish red to bleak black. Bits of animal bones, including chicken claws, long, shiny fangs and broken vertebrae, covered dried splotches of congealed blood and clumped gore, and situated at the head of the table, a large, open book.

Mansford gazed upon book's browning pages: neat, hand-written German on one page, the other featuring a wood-carved print of a Guaner galloping from out the gorged ground.

Instinct took over, and Mansford re-donned the mask. When next he looked, he understood the words.

"'For any conquest to assume form,'" he read, the words etching onto his brain, "'it must encompass every land, enrapture all inhabitants whether rich or poor, so that they may align with the Great Beast. The deity's servants may be demon or mortal, so long as they are willing to embrace the concepts of chaos to overthrow the status quotient. If but one track of land, one stretch of country remains untainted, victory cannot be attained. At all costs, the process must be merciless, widespread, and above all, its agents must strike fast, for the pious will be too contented to see what flanks them. They will not summon the urge to fight until it is too late, and it is for that very reason, the Guaner creed shall succeed.'"

Indignant voices approached. Mansford had to act fast. He placed his palms atop the pages, absorbing them from left-to-right and downward, devouring translucent layer upon layer, then once his mind had been crammed, he looked up and watched as the guard pushed his way in, while Murphy attempted to pull him back.

"I don't give a damn who he is," the guard sputtered. "He's not supposed to be in there. Mister Pickwick gave strict orders. If you're not willing to make it worth my while, then you'll just have to—"

The guard's mouth dropped, as he beheld the radiant face.

"Hush," Mansford ordered and waved Murphy inward, wiggling his fingers in such a way to signal him to shut the door, and then to the guard said, "Sit down."

The guard began to blabber, but in no precise words. He pulled out the chair nearest the door and flopped into it, quivering as tears streamed his face.

Mansford, now more Persona than mere mortal, waved his hand across the table, then around again, settling his finger on the unhinged man.

"Were you aware of such unorthodox activity taking place in this museum?" he asked the guard, while Murphy moved against the side wall, his expression deadpan.

"What...what activity?" he asked, his bleary eyes aimed beyond the unsavory items, allowing Mansford to pluck a series of petty crimes from his mind and flash them back. "I don't know what you mean. I just wanted an easy-going job. I got a criminal record, you know, served time. It's hard to get hired when you got yourself a record. Mister Pickwick's my boss. He calls the shots. I do what he says, like any good employee would."

"When did this particular gathering take place?" the Persona asked.

"Mister Pickwick's entourage comes and goes all the time here," the guard said. "I suppose they even come at night sometimes if something's big enough, but I swear, I don't work the night shift. The museum closes at six."

"Name these people who come and go," the Persona demanded.

"I don't know," the guard sniffled. "Honestly, I don't."

The Persona clenched his fists and rose, soaring across the table, rattling glass and bone from the surface.

"Ahhhh," the guard gasped, shutting his eyes.

The Persona touched down before him. "Come now," he said. "There must be at least one name you can share."

The guard cracked his lids. "Okay, all right, I'll tell you." He wet his lips, swallowed hard. "I've seen the librarian…Carmine Pascale. He's probably here more than at the library, and oh…Pickwick's wife. She comes here a lot, too."

The Persona tapped his shiny chin. "I take it she visits during her lunch hour."

The guard shrugged. "I don't keep tabs. She seems to do what she wants. She's been here with Pascale, even with the other men during their meetings, but I figured she was just helping with the catering and such." He glanced at the gruesome spread and frowned. "Okay, it was probably more than that." He closed his eyes again. "I've told you all I know. Please… please let me go."

"Very well," said the Persona, turning to Murphy, who budged from the wall to pull the guard up from the chair and shoved him from the room.

The Persona, meanwhile, sifted through the information he had gathered and from such, churned a brush of mental imagery: business men and women entering the chamber, donning robes, taking their seats. He saw Pickwick at the front, standing before the book, smirking as he opened it, mouthing its insidious words; Pascale standing at his side; a gray-haired woman as well, her features obscured by the sharp slope of her hood.

Small, dead animals, birds, chickens, rodents and others too mutilated to discern, were strewn about the table, and those gathered proceeded to slash the carcasses with their tiny spikes, while others crushed and twisted their little bodies, squeezing out their blood, muscles and bones into the pitchers, layering such with ample sums of the herbs and spices, which spewed a nauseating stench.

They slid the fullest pitchers toward Pickwick, and he in turn, poured the contents into a brass bottle and capped it.

"We might need more," said Pascale, "if we want to cover the required radius."

"No," said Pickwick. "This will do. We have so little time to spare."

The participants then rose: Pickwick, the hooded woman and Pascale leading the way from the chamber, their spectral shapes shooting past the Persona like fading images in a dream.

"You all right?" asked Murphy.

Mansford looked down from the table with mask now in hand. He wiped the sweat from his brow, widened his eyes and said, "Yes…couldn't be better, in fact." He leapt down. "We should go, officer."

"Sure," said Murphy, cognitive that something strange had just occurred and yet possessing no urge to question it. "Whatever you say."

Mansford strapped the mask onto his arm, and with Murphy exited the room and headed downstairs.

The guard stood quaking near the men's room, his hands braced against the tiled fringe, mumbling, "Forgive me…Forgive me." He then turned as Mansford and Murphy approached. "I didn't mean to do bad things in my life…never meant to turn a blind eye."

Mansford gave the man a compassionate pat, but continued on, for he knew, just as Pickwick had so assessed, there was little time to spare.

(XIV)

"**I** suppose we head to the library," Murphy said.

Mansford turned the corner. "I've a hunch there's no need."

"You sure?" Murphy asked. "Maybe it's best to err on the side of caution. At least very least, let me to have a look."

Mansford's mind was still swarming with thoughts and ideas, an impulse that told him to return to the penthouse, check on Standish.

"Sure, fine," said Mansford. "I'll drop you off, make a quick run home, then pick you back up."

"No need. The station's within walking distance. I have an extra uniform in my locker, and it really won't hurt me to start the shift early. I'll call you once I'm there."

"Sounds like a plan," Mansford agreed. "I'll give you my direct number."

"Again no need. We have it on file. We do that for the big-wigs around town: you, the mayor…Carl Clive. It's presumed you're vulnerable to

Mansford gave the man a compassionate pat…

crackpots who, if the opportunity were to arise, might take advantage. Yep, if we need to call, you're at our fingertips."

"That's reassuring," said Mansford, though his lack of enthusiasm was evident.

They drove without exchange to the library, and Mansford parked before its lofty, concrete steps.

"You okay with this?" Mansford asked, feeling guilty for his haste. "I could go along, if you'd want."

"I'm fine," Murphy argued. "Just going to investigate the surroundings."

"And what do you plan to tell your captain? To put it lightly, you've experienced, well, let's just say, some fairly extraordinary things."

"Extraordinary ain't the word," Murphy laughed, opening the door. "Listen, the way I figure, Mister Mansford, I could very well wake up from all this and that'll be that. For the time being, I've no qualms just to see it through. I mean, why spoil the fun?"

Mansford smiled, and Murphy gave him an affable salute, closed the door and ascended the steps.

Indeed, Mansford thought, what an adventure it was turning out to be: so full of danger, intrigue and of course, instinct. The latter was, indeed, most prevalent, since so much seemed to be riding on his intuitive decisions. He could only hope his mystical transformation would pave the required way, keep him on track, and if not...

"Hello," said Surrogate, materializing next to him.

Mansford jumped and regarded the specter's smoky face.

"What in..." he exclaimed. "Where'd you come from?"

Surrogate collected his thoughts. "I'll have you know, I've been nearby the entire time, keeping an eye on you and those you've enlisted; astute choices, I must say." He settled back in his seat, looking more at ease. "Indeed, you're doing a splendid job, considering you were thrown into this so quickly. Your symbiotic relationship with the mask is moving without a hitch...so far. Yes, you two appear a good match, but then you were the best candidate to don it."

"Nice of you to say." Mansford was still unsure of the specter's intent, but trusting it was positive. "So, any advice on my next step, or should I just let my intuition flow?"

"You evidently have a destination in mind. I say, seek it. Why contemplate the matter? After all, it's unwise to waste time."

Mansford nodded, but was still thirsty for answers. "Am I wrong to think that, somewhere down the line, this will all turn out for the best?"

"What's it matter? You know what you have to do. You wouldn't have taken the steps to advance your little convention. Your gala will spawn positive press for the mayor. Of course, his opponent's campaign declaration is definitely a prelude to a greater fight."

"So it won't be easy."

"With the Great Beguiler, how could it be otherwise? You read the excerpt. A Guaner must engage the opposition, especially if it holds leadership status. Such dire circumstances have gone on for years, often in secret but always resulting in skirmishes, often all-out wars. It's the Guaner style, if you will. A Guaner has no purpose unless it rocks the boat, causes conflict, fills foolish people's heads with trickery. This current one will surely prove exceptionally conniving, as will its followers, whether human or disguised denizen. Yes, you figured it right; they do change shape. That's why you must gather your resources fast. Your opponent will count on good people sitting idly by, for evil attains its goal when others remain passive, despite the evidence it plants."

"Is that why Pickwick displayed those statures: a subtle way to introduce his agenda, perhaps?"

"Of course; a basic warm-up to the shape of things to come," Surrogate added. "Those relics are putrid symbols of the beast's misguided pride. The Beguiler relishes such imagery, but will also distort its meaning as it furthers its crusade."

Mansford considered other current signs, the swastika and hammer-and-sickle: lurid symbols erected not to benefit humanity, as false promises claimed, but rather to corral and confine it.

"A great beguiler, indeed," Mansford said with distaste. "Nothing unsettles me more than those who twist the truth."

"As with me," concurred Surrogate, but as Mansford paused at a light, the specter began to fizzle. "Oh, my, it appears I've again overspent my time."

Mansford watched Surrogate's frame crackle of bright, electrical light.

"Fear not, Mister Mansford," his voice warbled, "I shall return."

Then…*poof*…he was gone, leaving Mansford to swerve onto the road that would lead him home, but if time was, indeed, of the essence, was a restful stop appropriate? Yet Surrogate knew what his intention was, or at least did not suggest he do anything contrary. In this regard, perhaps embracing impulse was the best way. Maybe it would lead him to something bigger, something brimming of further revelation.

In any event, the only way he would know was to follow his nose, and with Surrogate in evident hiding, he was more than intent in doing just that.

(XV)

T he air smelled peculiar as he drove toward the complex, sort of the way a baby does after messing itself.

As he neared, he noticed three men pacing along the front doors, handing out flyers to those who either entered or exited, and before the outer bushes, their signs were posted: BEN GYLER...A COMMONER OF UNCOMMON STATURE; BEN GYLER...A HUMBLE MAN TO LEAD.

Mansford parked and approached, discerning that two of the men were tall, one considerably shorter than them, with yet another of dwarfish stature.

The middle-sized one glanced at Mansford and cringed, as if he feared his presence.

"Gentlemen," Mansford acknowledged, as he walked closer, not intending to take a flyer or even indulge in conversation. The subtle stench then grew, making him waver.

He, of course, knew who they were and took morbid pleasure in absorbing their doughy faces, thin eyebrows, sporadic fluffs of thick hair atop their crowns.

The middle man exteded a flyer. "Gyler for mayor," he croaked, his voice rough and rusty. "He's for the common man, not like Poindexter, who's only out for the affluent."

Mansford grabbed the carbon-paper and regarded the combination of its smudged slogans.

Through this, he gained a replay of his brief visit to Pickwick's house. He recalled the kitchen specimen, how it was wrought with worry, pressing itself against the door, forcing itself to burst and fade.

Mansford crumbled the sheet and tossed it back at the now disguised creature. "I've known Poindexter for years and would hardly call him 'for the affluent'."

"Don't be fooled," a tall man said. "He can't identify with us regular folk, with his high-class suit and tie and lofty way of speech. He's nothing but an out-of-touch charlatan."

"Guess I fall into the same classification," commented Mansford.

"Perhaps," said the other man, "but at least you don't overtax the working class. Now, you must agree, that ain't right."

"I'm not sure that's Mayor Poindexter's intent," Mansford rebutted with a wry grin.

"You lie," a small voice then shrieked. It was the dwarf. He tugged at Mansford's pant cuff. "You're right to say you're like him. You're greedy and self-centered. It's your insidious kind we need to uproot."

Mansford frowned and shook the dwarf loose, then pushed himself past the others, making his way toward the doors, which had just flung open.

Men marched out, the air reeking stronger as they snickered. Some were big, others average, a few puny, and from out the assortment, one in particular emerged, standing out not because he was in any way extraordinary, or even attractive or dashing, but in that he was so plain and unassuming.

His face was wrinkled, drawn, but not old, perhaps more so world-weary, as if the sun had weathered it. His eyes were pale-blue, almost gray, softened with humility, while his hair was tinged white on the sides, but brushed back with a subtle panache that implied he may have once been a woman's fancy. His shirt was faded blue, his pants faded black, his shoes frayed and scuffed.

He regarded Mansford's attire with a disdainful smile.

"Hello," he reached out, "I'm Ben Gyler. In case you haven't heard, I'm running for mayor. May I count on your vote this November?"

Mansford kept his hands at his side and with a sly smirk replied, "Sorry, but I'm a Poindexter man; so are most of the folks in this vicinity. You'd be wise to carry your campaign elsewhere."

Insolent murmurs emerged, like the overlapping croaks of belligerent frogs, but Gyler raised his hand, gesturing them to hush.

"Of course, it's hard to switch teams when you're accustomed to the same one," the candidate explained, "but often you'll find a little change can do the soul good."

"Soul?" asked Mansford. "I was under the impression, demons were devoid of them."

More angry murmurs followed, and the dwarf sprinted over, once again latching onto Mansford's leg, this time tugging harder.

"Shut up, rich boy," he shouted, his ripe, doughy face turning beet red. "Shut up. We all know it's the affluent who are devoid of souls."

Mansford kicked the little guy away and again began to push his way through, but to do so he had to plow through Gyler.

His fingers grazed the pseudo-man's mushy chest, and as the sight of the rearing cemetery beast re-entered Mansford's mind, a sudden spurt of unintentional truth broke from his opponent's pliable face: nostrils widening, mouth curling, and beneath his orbs, two dimples where there would be additional ones, concealed only by translucent layers of synthetic skin.

Mansford raised his arm, the mask beaming through the dark cloth, making Gyler reel and resume his everyman guise. He looked hurt, confused...unappreciated, much to his entourage's collective lament.

Mansford skidded into the lobby, the day guard too immersed in a flyer's hollow claims to notice him.

Mansford hopped onto the elevator, wondering what may have transpired while the ghoulish gang was inside. Had they gone up to the penthouse?

He dashed into the hall, just as Sutton shut the door.

"Holy smokes," said the older man, "where have you been? Figured I'd head back to the cemetery. Stacey's gotten real tired...worn out like you wouldn't believe. My heart goes out to the poor girl. She told me some pretty amazing things."

"Worn out?" Mansford asked. "Really...that bad, huh?"

"Well, it didn't help that it took us eons to make it up here," said Sutton. "At first, that dopey guard was too preoccupied with our visitors to let us in, but better we wait in the hall, I thought, then among those creeps. Brother, were they ever all over the place, traveling up to every floor, knocking on every door. They were right on top of us, Mike, wouldn't let us breathe. Thank goodness your door was open."

"I see," Mansford said, reaching for the knob. "Come clean with me, Phil. Did they lay a hand on either of you?"

Sutton reached over, guiding his boss' hand downward. "She's fine, really, just winded, Mike. She's resting in your bed, trying to sleep off the commotion. She told me about that wild beast or whatever the hell it was. Anyway, she's thinks these creeps are part of that same crazy clique. Can't say I blame her. They're sure a slick bunch, especially the one dressed like a bum, going on with his you-owe-me-something propaganda. Can you believe that jerk is running for mayor?"

"Yes, Phil, I know. Hard to fathom."

"He's a phony all right," Sutton said. "You can see it in his stance, the way he tries to be Mister Common. His true colors came through, though, when he was leering at Stacey, licking his lips, undressing her with his eyes." Sutton shook his head, clicked his tongue. "Yeah, sure…man of the people, my foot."

"I appreciate the details, Phil, but please, I need to see for myself she's okay." He reached again for the knob. "Now if you don't mind."

Sutton sensed the extent of his friend's tension and let him enter, following him inside.

Mansford peered into the bedroom and saw Standish sprawled on her back across the bed, her eyes shut, her body heaving in her bra and panties, her skin gleaming of sweat. She looked ill, both inside and out.

He dashed to her side and patted her hand as Sutton rolled his eyes.

"She was cognitive when I left," Sutton said. "She said good-bye, sounded just fine, but like I said, Mike, she's real tired."

Standish sensed him and opened her eyes. "Oh," she whispered, "it's… it's you, Mike." She then looked at Sutton. "And Phil…I…I thought you had gone."

"Never mind us," said Mansford. "How are you feeling?"

"All right, I suppose," she said, raising herself up, "except…" She rubbed her temple. "I do sense a headache coming on."

"Phil, go to the medicine cabinet. Get some aspirin…a glass of water."

Sutton grumbled, but obliged.

Mansford guided her face back to his and inspected her eyes. "You look drugged, my dear. I wonder if the effects of that chloroform is lingering."

"Don't be silly," she said, but as he probed deeper, another vision entered his head. He saw the amber-hued hall, Sutton standing at her side, trying to pull her away, while Gyler entranced her, his lips locked, but his voice droning: "The time of change has come, Miss Standish. You and your family will surely benefit from it. Look around. This opulence here can be shared: a portion placed in your very pocket. Your father works hard, doesn't he? So does your mother. So do you and Mister Pascale. Why hob-knob with silver-spoon inheritors, when you can gain the most illustrious treats through avenues plain and simple? Discard this playboy masquerader. Make him stumble as he promotes his incompetent crony and in the end, I'll have you join me on stage, on that glorious night when I embrace my role as Brink Town's new mayor."

Mansford saw Gyler's face twisting, wavering, as Sutton shoved him back and shook his fist, forcing the trickster and his entourage into the elevator. They regarded the older man with smug contempt as the doors swooshed shut, and then the vision ceased.

"No surprise," Mansford stroked her brow. "He tried to put a spell on you. Thank God you have a strong constitution. Lesser individuals would have sooner succumbed." He looked deeper into her eyes. "Yes, I'm sure you're clear."

Sutton returned with the aspirins and water. She took them, handed the glass back and placed her cheek upon Mansford's shoulder.

"In a way," she admitted, "I feel worse than I did last night. I'm scared, worried. Something terrible is happening, I fear. I wonder how many others sense it, how many others it might effect." She fluttered her lashes, squirmed. "My mother, Mike...did you...?"

Mansford frowned. "We're still working on it. We'll have some info soon." He then laid her down. "Don't worry, Stacy. Close your eyes, rest. Contrary to the way it may seem, everything's under control."

She sighed and did as instructed.

Sutton slid the glass onto the night table, and the men exited, but as soon as Mansford shut the door, Sutton snapped, "We got this under control? You honestly believe that, Mike?"

With a stern squint, Mansford contemplated the matter and then tapped his elbow. "But of course," he said, "in every way imaginable," to which a barrage of rebellious shouts then broke from outside.

"What in the...?" Sutton gasped.

They dashed to the window, drew back the blinds and looked down on the mass of people, with more entering from the sidelines. A couple dwarfs carted a soap box inward and atop it, with old-time movie director mega-phone in hand; Gyler hopped atop and motioned for silence.

"Look at him," Sutton declared, "grandstanding. What's the point? He should take his damn sheep elsewhere."

"He wants to rub it in," Mansford suggested. "This, you see, is his way of challenging me."

"Ladies and gentlemen," Gyler bellowed into the cone, his voice laced with homespun sincerity, "I'm so pleased you could gather here today. As you're aware, I'm ramming in my figurative stake, making it known to one and all, I intend be Brink Town's mayor."

Cheers and claps followed. A few folks even hoisted their cardboard signs, jutting them toward Mansford's window.

"Thank you, thank you," said Gyler, slapping his chest. "I appreciate your support. Truly I do, but there's more I need to share."

Mansford slid the mask from his arm, raising it to his head, his gestures so smooth, so silent, that Sutton remained unaware. He then looked down, regarding the ever expanding crowd, and as Gyler continued speaking, he peered past the charlatan's fake skin, absorbing his hideous hide, as well as those of the varying sized specimens that flanked him.

"There are many at the top," railed Gyler, raising his arms in exasperation, while keeping the cone near his lips; the shadowy hint of two more additional arms bouncing from beneath as he did so. "They come in many styles, from various heritages and hold a variety of devout beliefs." He legs stiffened as he centered himself upon the crate, the imprints of his additional legs dangling at the sides. "Sure, they don't care if you follow a different path, so long as you help them maintain their cozy mansions and luxurious cars, dine in the finest restaurants, land their planes on exotic shores. Yeah, folks, you know how it goes. You see evidence of it every day."

Those nearest him nodded their knobby heads, clapped their clawed hands.

"Some are Jewish, some German, Irish, Russian, Chinese, Japanese... Italian," Gyler went on, his rubbery face creaking. "They pretend they're like us, that they can identify with us, that they honestly care, but they know nothing of our plights, nothing whatsoever of what it means to work, to earn a measly dollar, only then to have it swiped away for the sake of another's greed."

Those nearest him then subtly moved among those who were clearly human, patting their backs, whispering insidiously into their ears, their false words ascending, filtering through the mask, into Mansford's astute consciousness.

"Why work any harder for that proverbial piece of the pie, my friends?" Gyler, the Great Beguiler, proclaimed, sneaking a sinewy arm across his chest. "You've invested in it, nurtured it, kept it alive and well all these years. Is it now wrong to reach out, request the return of that which is yours?" He smiled, his slimy teeth beaming through. "However, to make this click, I sure do need your help, and I'm not talking about your loose change, but rather your time and effort and above all, your unconditional belief. Join me, my fellow citizens, wherever you can, whenever you want, for establish stations across this good town to reveal Poindexter for the money-hording pawn that he is." He pointed into the crowd, his flabby fingers gesturing someone toward him. "You only need to give your name, address and number to my campaign manager, and he'll guide you from there. Come on, Jon...let these good people see who you are."

Up to the miniature stage, Pickwick swaggered, his movements curt, rushed, his eyes aimed up at the penthouse window. He extended his hand, shook the creature's, at which point the monster hunkered off the box, allowing the curator to assume his place.

Into the megaphone, Gyler blared, "Mister Jon Pickwick, ladies and gentlemen... You may know him from your favorite museum...have surely seen him on more than occasion over the years. Yes, that's right, he runs the whole show there, setting up displays, collecting artifacts, giving informative tours, helping to educate you and your children, and you know what? He firmly believes in our crusade. Go 'head. Tell them, Jon."

The beast tossed Pickwick the cone, and with quivering hand, he positioned it near his mouth, his eyes still aimed upward.

"That's right, Ben," Pickwick began, his words starting soft but mounting as his courage increased, "I've come to my senses, seen the light. Yes, I make a decent salary, Ben, and yes, in more than a good many years, I've done financially well, but my concern for my family's welfare has still prevailed, if only due to the questionable things I've learned. Let me tell you, my friends, I've attended more than a few high-end parties over time. I've witnessed the waste, heard all the crass comments. In other words, I know the cretins who run this town, know their unscrupulous tactics, and let me tell you, they sure ain't pretty."

Applause-laced laughter passed through the crowd, the henchmen continuing to rub elbows with what outsiders they could, intent in convincing them that what they heard was true.

"I've met Percival Poindexter on more than several occasions," said Pickwick, his gaze now locked on Mansford's pearly persona, his words flowing fast. "I've often heard him speak his mind. He's not a bad man per say, just out of line with the times, influenced by those who line his pockets for favors in exchange. Now, I don't know about you, but I often do hunger for a bigger slice of that pie. After all, I helped back it, just like you, and to say I can't have a mere nibble is just wrong. Ben Gyler knows that feeling all too well. Indeed, I've encountered many kinds of people in my time...good, bad and otherwise...and Ben Gyler is...no ifs, ands or buts... definitely our kind. Sure, he may have come out of left field, but that's only because he's lived an unassuming life like the rest us. How many people know you, but that doesn't make you any less for your obscurity, correct? Well, what's important is that Ben Gyler identifies with us, cares about us and will always fight for our concerns, because, my fellow citizens, our concerns are his concerns." He took a deep breath. "I...I thank you."

Pickwick then closed his eyes, dropped the megaphone, hobbled back into the crowd, leaving Gyler to gaze up in his place, his massive head cocked: cool, steady and cruel.

Mansford did not flinch, recalling scenarios based on what he had learned from the text: of desperate lands where monsters cloaked themselves as men and inspired the masses to forge blades, guns and promises that left only blood and death in their wake.

"That's right," Mansford swore, "I now not only know what you are, but how you operate, and by the time I'm through, so will everyone."

Sutton glanced over, only then noticing Mansford's mask and stepped to the side, while below, the crowd dispersed. Gyler waddled from out them, leading both man and beast beyond the vicinity.

As Mansford removed his disguise, he regarded not only Sutton, but much to his surprise, Standish, as well.

"Where'd you come from?" Sutton asked, again taken aback by her revealing form, but her eyes acknowledged only Mansford, or rather the shiny object he grasped.

"I heard noises from outside," she said, smacking her lips, blinking from the mask's mesmerizing refraction, "and heard Mike's voice, but in an oh-so-different tone...and of course, before that, there was Gyler's." She shivered, raised her gaze to his. "Beneath the surface, I could clearly hear it...so manipulative...so inhuman."

Mansford placed the mask atop the desk and led her back to the bedroom. "Push it all out of your head, my dear. If you wish to rid yourself of that headache, you should rest."

Mansford closed the door behind them, and in the process tripped, falling upon her. In confusion, she turned, stared at him, and in answer, she leaned forward, but Mansford kept her at bay.

"It's probably as well I be going now," Sutton said from outside the door. "I've sure had my fill of weirdness for one day. You know, now that I think about it, maybe I should just stop listening to those crazy radio shows about masked crime-fighters and such. Though I must say, I've read some of that stuff's actually based on fact...still a bad influence, I suppose." He laughed, as the couple stiffened. "Well, Mike, I suppose you'll be in touch with Murphy, though what that hot-shot does is of little consequence to me. If he was smart, he'd get his entire precinct involved, but then again, what do I know?" Standish leaned nearer and moaned. "Okay, then...I'll, uh, call ya later...okay? Unless there's something else you need me to do?"

"No, no," Mansford replied. "Everything's fine, Phil." He led Standish toward the bed. "We'll talk soon, and at length, I promise."

Sutton then left, slamming the front door behind him, much to Mansford's relief.

"Good gracious," he grumbled. "I thought he'd never leave." He sat Standish down. "Now, really you've got to rest." He searched her dreamy eyes. "I'm really starting to worry about you."

She smiled, then threw her arms around his shoulders and upon his lips, planted a long, breathy kiss.

He did not resist, even though he knew he should, with the mask right in the other room, prickling at his conscience. How could he, though, considering he now embraced a woman for whom many a man would have sold his soul.

They rolled onto the mattress, kissing, hugging. She removed her bra, signaling there was then no turning back. Into the deep, black regions of sinful consummation, where virginal sanctity held no claim, they plunged.

(XVI)

The best Mansford uttered was "Forgive me," as much to himself as the young lady, not that she heard. She was fast asleep, her body coiled against his.

How many hours had passed? Why did his mind feel so sluggish, so empty?

The phone rang, and he assumed it was Sutton, perhaps even Murphy. He reached over to the night table and fingered the receiver.

"Hello…" he whispered.

"Mike…that you?" Clive asked. "Say, you don't sound well. You sick?"

"No, was just taking a nap," Mansford voiced a trifle louder, watching Standish twitch and turn toward the other side of the bed. "So, whatcha got for me?"

"A witchy woman with gray hair is what I've got," Clive said. "She stopped by about twenty minutes ago, dropped off the check, per the MCC, through Brink Town Banking. It's signed by its campaign chief, Jon Pickford, along with a little extra as a down payment for the next Gyler ad."

"Well, I'll be…Did you accept it?"

"Better part of wisdom told me not to, but I figured in this instance, maybe it was wise to play along. I don't have to cash the damn thing, you know, and I certainly don't have to run the stupid ad this very instant." He paused. "So, you got dirt on these people? If so, please share. I don't know how fast my reporters can dig it up, and I really can't wait forever to make a decision on this, though I suppose it's wiser to squash it sooner than later."

"Yes, squash it immediately," Mansford insisted. "I'm still compiling the dirt, as it were, but you're just going to have to trust me on this, Carl. These characters are far worse than you might imagine."

"No problem, Mike. Consider it done."

"Beyond the gray hair and the witchy look, anything else discerning about the woman?"

"I must say, she did look familiar, like I've seen her around…maybe at the bank, the school board…the library, perhaps. Still, I've no particular reason to know the old wench."

"No, I suppose not. Just trying to get a better handle."

"Well, if I learn anything further, I'll give you a holler, and you do vice-versa for me, hear?"

"You got it, Carl. Thanks for the scoop."

"Anytime, pal."

Mansford felt the impulse to dial the police station, see if Murphy had arrived by chance, but when he saw Standish squirm, he hung up, grabbed his robe and returned to his desk, where another phone, and of course, the mask, awaited.

As he asked the operator to connect him, he regarded his pearly possession, noticing that, though it still shined, it had lost some of its luster, or was it a trick of the light? He picked the mask up, studied it. No, it did seem a tad duller…but why?

"Oh, hello," he said, as a woman asked how she might assist. "I'm Michael Mansford. I was hoping that Officer Jack Murphy was available." He turned the mask from side-to-side, hoping to rekindle its luster. "Oh, I see… Really? So, he never showed up for his shift, you say…Why, yes, please do tell him I called when he arrives. He evidently knows how to get in touch with me…Yes, I'd certainly appreciate that… Thank you… You have a good day, too."

He put the receiver down, continuing to angle the mask.

"Forgive me, indeed," he whispered, then glanced through the crack of the bedroom door, at Standish's milky frame. "I sure did wrong, didn't I?" He glanced back at the mask, feeling guilty and unsure. "I mean, if what I did is the cause, please give me a little time, won't you? I'm sure I can redeem myself, set this thing straight."

The mask shimmered, but again, only subtly.

Without further ado, he snuck back into the bedroom, pulled a fresh outfit from the closet, tiptoed out, strapped the mask back onto his arm and made another quick call.

"Hello there, Timmon's Dress Shop…This is Michael Mansford. I have a request…There's a young lady at my suite who's in need of some attire, tailor-fit, if that can be arranged…No, it's not for Miss James… Nevertheless, if someone might be so kind to come by with a few samples, I'd greatly appreciate it. Incidentally, I believe small is the size…Very well, and as always, thank you."

He hung up, then pulled some scrap paper from the drawer and penned: "*Stacy…Must rush out again. We'll chat. I promise you that. A lady from the dress shop will stop by, give you something that fits. Don't be shy. Let her in. She'll announce herself at the door. Otherwise, please be cautious. Be back as soon as I can.*"

He propped the note at the base of the small lamp and then dashed out.

● ● ●

Mansford entered the library and spotted a hawkish looking, old woman with bright-dyed red hair at the front desk, flipping through a periodical. She seemed a hard sell, but he donned a smile and approached.

"Hello, how are you today?" he asked, layering on the charm.

She glanced up, expressionless.

"I'm Michael Mansford," he contineud hoping such might work some influence. "I'm looking for a police officer. He visited your establishment a couple hours ago. There isn't a chance he might still be around, is there?"

"Officer?" she said and glanced back at the magazine, flipping another page. "I don't recall seeing any officer."

"Well, that's understandable. He was in civilian dress, but I was thinking perhaps he made his presence known, perhaps even showed his badge." He noticed a few people stationed at the surrounding tables, glancing up from their books. "Perhaps he conversed with some of these folks. Would you mind if I asked?"

"This is a library, sir. These people are here for peace and quiet…to read, not be interviewed. Now, unless you need assistance with a particular title…"

"Yes, in fact, I do," Mansford thought quickly. "I'm looking for information on a mythical beast…one called the Guaner." He smiled. "Any suggestions?"

She frowned, pointed to the right. "The card catalog is to your right."

"Thank you." Mansford headed toward a series of steel cabinets.

He stepped toward the "title/subject" section, opened the "G" drawer, and of course, found nothing. He sighed, intent to move on when from the side, someone hissed.

He saw a pretty brunette, dressed in plaid attire at the end of the aisle. She rolled her eyes, waved him toward her and then disappeared to the left.

Mansford followed, catching her mid-way down the center row in the Science Fiction section. Again she rolled her eyes, waved and stepped backward, until she pressed against the far brick wall.

"Yes, young lady," Mansford asked, noticing her nervous state. "What can I do for you?"

"It's more a matter of what I can do for you, Mister Mansford," she whispered with unintentional suggestiveness, then explained, "I couldn't help but overhear your exchange." She peered over his shoulder before continuing. "My name's Cindy Cartel. I work here. I have to be careful not to get in any trouble, you see. I do need this job, but I must tell you, Miss Birdsley wasn't exactly on the level with you."

"Hmmm…in what way would you say?"

"A policeman was here, Mister Mansford, plain clothes, of course, and he did show his badge from what I saw. He even chatted at length with Ms. Standish, the head librarian, and then Mister Pascale came over. The three of them headed toward the back. Ms. Standish returned, rounded us up and told us not to say anything to anyone about the matter, no matter who they were, since it was some sort of official business. She came down particularly hard on Miss Birdsley, I must say, and even though Miss Birdsley doesn't particularly like Ms. Standish, she always follows her instructions to the tee. I mean we all do. We don't want to get fired."

"I can appreciate that," said Mansford. "Tell me, Cindy, is Ms. Standish here now? I'd like to talk to her. I promise to be discreet."

"Oh, she's definitely gone," said the young woman, her eyes widening. "She gave us our orders, then left with Mister Pascale. I'm assuming the policeman was with them. I'm really not sure if Ms. Standish is coming back, either. Maybe her daughter might know since she's scheduled for today." She glanced at her watch. "She really should have been here an hour ago, though. Seems rather doubtful now."

"I see." Mansford was thinking of his amorous tryst with Stacey. He was tempted to don the mask, to gain additional insight, but restrained himself. "You said the three headed toward the back. Can you show me?"

The young lady shrugged and scooted around him. "Not sure how precise I can be, though I'm guessing they probably headed into the employee parking lot." She skipped to the end of the aisle, looked both ways and signaled him onward.

They came to the rear door, upon which LIBRARY STAFF ONLY was stenciled. The young woman glanced behind her, then sensing the coast

"Mrs. Birdsley wasn't…on the level with you."

was clear, pushed the bar handle to open the door just enough to grant Mansford a decent shot of the lot.

"Miss Standish's car is gone," she acknowledged, "Mister Pascale's, too." She pointed to the far end, where a long gate was ajar. "We usually take turns closing the gate on the honor-system. So much for that. I guess they were in a hurry."

Mansford spotted a trickle of blood surrounding the two empty spots and commented, "I assume that's where Standish and Pascale were parked."

"Sure, goes to reason," the young lady replied, also noticing the bloody trail. "Gosh, sure looks like someone got hurt, doesn't it?"

"Yes, it does," Mansford acknowledged, allowing her to close the door, "and I dread to think to what extent, particularly on the poor officer's end."

"You think Miss Standish and Mister Pascale are up to no good?" the young lady asked with morbid cheer. "I always thought they were kind of shifty...kind of devilish, that is."

"I'm not at liberty to say," Mansford answered, but his taut expression confirmed her suspicion.

"I'll be darn," she said. "I guess I'm safe, then."

"Safe?" asked Mansford. "What do you mean?"

"From losing my job. I mean, if they're in the wrong, and I've went against orders."

Mansford smiled. "Listen, if anyone should have an inclination to fire you," he said, pulling out his wallet and handing her his business card, "you give me a call, and that's goes for anyone else here, including grouchy ole' Miss Birdsley."

"Gee whiz, thanks," the young lady exclaimed. "Wait till my friends see this—Michael Mansford's personal number. Wow...they'll be ever so envious."

Mansford laughed, perhaps regretting his generosity all too late, then told her, "I'm heading out this way. I don't want to draw anymore attention to myself than is necessary." He placed his finger to his lips. "Mums the word, now, Cindy...promise?"

"Yes, Mister Mansford," she giggled, "I promise, sir...not a word."

Mansford's gaze revisited the blood and the two sets of tire tracks that stemmed from such, which faded into the asphalt, making it impossible to say whether they had turned left or right.

He caressed the mask, hoping he might renew its magical vigor; at best and most, his mind only tingled.

Discouraged, he made his way to the front of the building, hopped dejectedly into his car, cursing himself for having been so impulsive. A man his age, he thought, ought to be ashamed. What in the world was he thinking, having his way with such a young, innocent lass…and one in extreme peril, no less?

He revved the engine, and in a desperate attempt to pacify his self-degradation, turned on the radio, catching the end of Rimsky-Korsakov's "Flight of the Bumblebee." Mansford then listened as the Green Hornet's narrative intro commenced, followed by the radio announcer reporting the start of a special encore presentation of last week's broadcast adventure…

With this, he headed down the road, his ears pricked as he drove, for it was easy to identify with such a hero: a wealthy gent of inherited wealth, who despite his playboy lifestyle, remained racked by an insatiable urge to do good.

To supplement his romantic rumination, Mansford gained the oddest, most inspiring notion of how he might get back on track, and though the better part of wisdom told him he should visit the precinct, he chose Esoteric, instead.

It was there, and only there, he was assured he could revitalize the mask's magical properties, thus regaining his required momentum, but this time, he would elevate his mission to a more purposeful level.

(XVII)

"**P**erfect timing," said Stark, placing the box upon his work table. "Just got it ready, in fact. Now, you should realize, it may appear slapped-together on the surface, but I must say, it's quite practical, considering it was no easy task to modify the basic material."

Mansford tugged his ear. "Okay, already, Ned, let's see it."

Stark grinned and pulled forth a large, black, bra-like cup.

"Ta-da," he chimed, propping it before his chest. "So, what do you think?"

"It's lovely," Mansford frowned, "except that…"

"Except what?"

"Are you sure it's sturdy? With all due respects…whatever it is…it doesn't look very strong."

Insulted, Stark lifted the object higher, then slammed it hard upon the table, causing a reverberating thud, then swung it back up.

"Take a good look, my friend," Stark said. "Not a scratch or dent on it." He slapped it like a drum. "Rock-solid, I'd say."

Mansford paused, wrinkled his nose and shrugged.

"It opens easy, too," Stark pressed the outer cusp, making the cup flip open. "The mask slips right into the velvety cushioning, which suctions it ever-so-slightly." Stark set the contraption down and reached back into the box and pulled out another. "To balance you out, this one can latch onto your opposite hip. As you can see, they'll function like holsters. They have metal hinges. You clip them right onto your belt. Heck, you can even pack a pistol in this one, maybe a knife if you want, and the nice thing is, neither one will obstruct your movements. You simply swing your arms nice and free, until you're ready."

"Impressive," Mansford commented. "How did you come up with the material?"

"If you recall a few years back, we were toying with some protective athletic gear for kids, figured we could distribute it to schools and various sporting clubs, but then the whole idea went off the deep end. I mean, come on, kids need a good dose of the ole' rough-and-tumble, even the gals." He shook his head. "It'll be a sad day, indeed, when we start depriving our youth of their mandatory cuts and bruises, but that's another complaint for another time." He chuckled. "Anyhow, for a grown man hankering for otherworldly adventure, it's a different deal. These babies were supposed to be shoulder pads, you know. I intensified layers of our old, cloth-strengthening fluid and presto-chango, another Esoteric miracle achieved."

Mansford pulled the first pad toward him, clicked it open, set it back down. He then removed the fabric from his elbow, then the mask and placed inside the dark, cushioned compartment.

"And here's a special belt I whipped up," added Stark, pulling a rolled, leathery band from the side. "It's made of the same material, but much more flexible. It'll snap on, be easier to wear that way."

"Nice." Mansford closed the pad and looped it onto the belt, while grabbing the other. He put the black, magnetic clasps from each end together, so that they clicked below his stomach. "I like this a lot, Ned." He tapped the left pad, and like a gunslinger drawing his pistol, swept the mask from out, right up to his face. "Yeah, this is definitely going to work."

Stark's expression, however, conveyed some uncertainty.

"What wrong?" asked Mansford, glancing through the eye holes.

"I don't know. You just don't look as…well, as majestic as I recall." He scoped Mansford over from head to toe. "Can't quite pinpoint it."

Mansford lowered the mask, too ashamed to admit his theory had faltered. Indeed, whatever magic Stark worked, it was not enough to rekindle the sheen.

Stark snapped his fingers. "Wait a minute…got an idea."

He ran behind the rubber-rat stack, flung open a creaky, old door and from inside it, grabbed a long, black coat.

"I know this may sound silly, but your dad used to wear this for masquerades, Halloween and the like." Sutton patted off the dust. "Despite its age, it's pretty spiffy: Edwardian, velvet-trimmed. For whatever odd reason, it's called a morning coat, but in my estimation, the dark content always relegated it more to night." He pointed to the left-side row of five, silver buttons, and lifted one of the cuffs to reveal four more. "Stylish, with just enough fine detail to set it off, but of course, you don't actually button it. The buttons are for looks; the whole coat is, in truth. You just keep it flapped open, and then when you're ready, reach for the hip."

"So," Mansford surmised "you think it would conceal the pads?"

"Adequately enough," replied Stark, "but I was thinking more along the lines of embellishing your overall mystique, especially when you wear the mask. We could, in fact, have a whole stash of these coats made up, for the sake of your public appearances, or whatever it is you might fancy. The combination would click beautifully. Even if someone spotted you in public in Edwardian gear, they'd just think it was because you're eccentric. No one would be the wiser. It's your image to be a tad off…mask and all."

Mansford reached over, fingered the fabric. "It's a tad thick for summer."

"For as long as you're probably going wear the thing, what's it matter? Keep it in the back seat of your Packard; fling it over your shoulder when you stroll through Brink Town Park. Slip it on whenever the moment feels right." Stark held it open. "So what do you say? Try it on?"

With nothing to lose, Mansford consented, this time strapping the mask onto his face and in turning, allowing Stark to guide his arms into the lush cloth. Stark then straightened it about his shoulders and after a few tugs. "How's that feel?"

Mansford did not answer, for he felt indifferent in his modified guise, though a tinge comforted in knowing his dear father had at least worn the garment. Nonetheless, as the seconds ticked, the coat's decades-laden aura washed over him, in a way becoming as much a part of his body as the mask, and somehow in the process, it made him feel buoyant.

"Sweet Mary," Stark declared, springing back. "What's this? Is it a trick of my eyes, or are you…oh, dear me…levitating?"

In truth, it mattered little, though, whether Mansford was, in fact, ascending, for his mind was anchored by mental weight, prompting him to relive his consummation with Standish, even at the point when he hit the ceiling. At that lofty stance, he recalled the young lady's sweet scent, and through it, could now decipher what he had been too blind prior to detect: a cascading blur of her childhood, devoid of love, encouragement, one father dying so that another could stand in lieu, this new one callous and cruel, denouncing anything pious and pure, keeping her more restrained than any religious zealot might have dared.

Above all else, it was her father's contempt for sanctity that enraged him, for any man who dared sacrifice his daughter, blood-related or not, was not a man, but a monster. In the same vein, Mansford realized, any man who would take advantage of a woman in the wake of such betrayal, was not much better. After all, to combat the Great Beguiler, it was imperative that one stay on a respectable level, or so his alter-ego reminded him.

Stark grabbed Mansford leg and pulled him down, the Edwardian coat flapping from some abrupt, internal gust, the mask flickering like a winded flame, while stacks of boxes teetered and fell. The mask then echoed as might a cycle in a carnival tunnel, swarming round and round, while its strap and bolts blurred, so that the disguise appeared one with Mansford's flesh: organic and plasmatic.

"Hold on," cried Stark, squinting. "I can't see. The light's too bright. You've got to help me here. Latch onto my arms."

Mansford obliged, until his heels touched the floor. The gust died, as did the mask's radiance.

Stark blinked, shook his head and focused on Mansford, who regarded him from behind the mask, his eyes dull and despairing.

"Oh, my," Stark gasped. "That was quite a stunt." He wiped his brow. "If we could find some way to bottle what propelled you, we'd make a million bucks. Then again, I've a hunch, not everyone's equipped to pull off such an amazing stunt."

Mansford nodded, uncertain if he or the Persona held control.

Stark studied the disguise. "It sure can sparkle, can't it?" He straightened Mansford's collar. "See? I knew the coat would be the good embellishment. I mean, look what happened when you put it on."

"You may be right," Mansford, muttered, removing the mask, his cognition thrusting against his brow as he joked, "I suppose, it's wise to make a first good impression, especially when one's face is concealed." He examined the mask, pleased it had regained at least some of its gleam. "Maybe this will get me back on track. It appears I slipped a while ago, Ned. I really need to remedy the matter."

Stark frowned. "Don't tell me…it was the girl, right?"

Stark's shrewdness impressed him.

"Heck," Stark tossed a few rats back into their boxes, "it's all right. I felt the guilt flowing from your mind, along with a bunch of other stuff. Strangest damn thing, but it was all pretty clear in the end. I guess wrong is wrong, Mike. Anyway, I hope whatever happened won't inspire you to live like a priest."

Mansford placed the mask into its protective cup, snapped it shut. "I'm not sure what to think, Ned...I'd assume the ladies are still worth pursuit, depending on the circumstances. I'm not so sure I'm up to the challenge here. It's something I've been pulled into by the grace of God, or so I'm presuming. Once it's settled, I'm sure my life will return to business as usual, along with all the general habits, good and bad." He paused, his words triggering his memory. "Speaking of such, how's the Gag Fest coming along?"

"Gag Fest? Oh yes. Somehow, I managed to get the Immaculate Conception Church Banquet Hall to comply for a small sum. Father Bruno also pulled a few strings to help it all along. He was surprised you'd allow the orphans to attend, but of course, he's not the only one there. Anyway, I called Percy. He's scheduled for a week's vacation this month, but for the sake of the event, said he'd definitely postpone it. Incidentally, he's quite aware of this out-of-the-blue competitor. He's scared some, but also figures the extra publicity could still paint him in a favorable light."

"And so, when exactly are we set?"

Stark grinned. "Two days from now. How's that for fast? I just have to finalize the catering, but such should be done by this evening."

"My, my," Mansford approved, "you truly are a miracle worker, Ned."

"Hey, I'm not the one flies toward the ceiling," Stark shot back. "I sure hope that whatever you're doing...whatever this phenomenon is...it works out for you. The air's been feeling real bad, my friend, almost apocalyptic, I'd say. I'm not a Biblical man, but I sure as hell hope this isn't our final days."

"I assure you, Ned, it isn't, not if I have any say in the matter...and that goes doubly for the Persona."

"The Persona," Stark rolled the name off his tongue. "Oh, I see...that'll be your code name. I like it. It's classy but creepy, like something one of those crusading radio heroes might use, though then again, most would probably add another word to the title, a color or something like that. You could incorporate the pearly sheen, of course."

"Not necessary," Mansford grumbled. "For now, brevity will simply suffice."

"Ah, sure, what's in a name?" Stark agreed. "It's the overall image that counts...and one's actions." He bit his lip, then offered, "Just be glad your instincts are guiding you, Mike. It was a wise choice to come back here. For example, Murphy won't be easy to track. You'll have to go around the bend a few times before you find him. It's best to lay the necessary groundwork first, get those little, important things out of the way."

"How'd you know about Murphy? I didn't mention him to you."

Stark threw up his hands. "Like I said, certain things flowed from your head. I guess I caught what I could, including that incidental tidbit. Sorry if I overstepped my bounds."

Mansford smiled. "No problem... I guess it's just par for the course. It's not easy to get a handle on this, sifting through all the strange particulars, that is." He glanced at the clock. "Anyway, time is of the essence. I should be pressing on." He reached over, grabbed Stark's hand and shook. "Thanks for your help, Ned." He spread his arms, extending the coat like it were a cape. "Indeed, this proved just the right touch."

"No problem," his friend said. "I'll keep you abreast on the fest. I'm going to call Clive next, see if he can plaster a few ads in tomorrow's paper. We certainly don't want to hide our little gala from the public."

"I've no doubt Clive will oblige," Mansford stepped around boxes, "but just to be on the safe side, get your staff to fashion some posters, list the date, time and where. With all due respects to the Brink Town Times, storefronts are always the best places to advertize. Oh, and don't be shy about adding some overtime for the staff. I'll be most distressed if those rats aren't ready."

Mansford then exited, happy to sport his antiquated coat, though gaining a few glances from the passing employees. He could not have cared less, though. As Stark had said, he was an eccentric and even more so, a fledgling avenger. Why not start to flaunt it?

However, when he was back on the road, his doubts mounted. He passed the precinct several times in fact, and felt compelled to question his actions. There had to be a quicker, more efficient means to locate Murphy, but with the Standish still preying on his mind, he decided to succumb to his instincts and steered home.

Perhaps after he apologized to her, informed her of all he had since learned and experienced in the passing hours, he could then attain a clearer perspective to carry on.

(XVIII)

Mansford entered the elevator just as Charlie stepped from his desk.

"Hey, Mister Mansford," he exclaimed. "You might like to know, the lady from the dress shop was here. She said she left a note at your door. By the way, sir, real spiffy coat."

"Oh, uh, yeah, thanks, Charlie." The doors started to shut. "Appreciate the heads-up. Chat with you later."

Mansford then ascended, curious as to why Standish did not let the woman in. He yanked the note from between the crack and whispered its words: "*Hello, Mr. Mansford. Stopped by about two. Sorry, but no one answered. Will visit later if you wish. Please call...Sincerely, Leslie Timmons.*"

Mansford sensed the worse and jaunted inside, toward the bedroom.

The bed was made. He looked about, hoping she was elsewhere, but in vain. Why had she left? How foolish.

"The damage is done," Surrogate's voice said from behind. "Alas, you'll have to take it in stride, make do without her."

He rose from the farther end of the bench, where the cheaper dummies were stationed.

"Right on time," said Mansford. "As you've probably guessed, I could have used your help a tad earlier."

"I didn't set these events in motion," Surrogate snapped and slid toward him. "You did that on your own." He frowned, causing the smoke to stream onto his chest. "I'm not sure if it was the basic consummation that threw things off, or the general waste of time, but evil always looks for an opportunity and never dilly-dallies. It forges perpetually ahead."

"I understand," Mansford confessed and in shame, turned from him. "I'll make amends, somehow. I'll...I'll find her, make everything right."

"As well as Officer Murphy, I suppose."

Mansford spun around. "You ought to know where he is," Mansford accused. "The same goes for Stacey. Why not share? If only out of decency, help me do my job, give me something to work with."

Surrogate bowed his head. "I'm only as good as you are, my friend. Yes, I do pick up on things, enough to guide you along from here to there if it's so ordained, but your actions dictate the terms. It's how the game is played."

"Then change the rules," Mansford insisted. "There's far too much at stake."

"I can't do that," said Surrogate, wringing his hands, "any more than I...or any one of my kind...can do so in Germany, Italy...Japan. My sect only watches, suggests, and if things get too out of hand...if one of our disciples should shrug the cause...that's on him. The problem is, once circumstances slip...even to the slightest degree...it's difficult, if not impossible, to harness the consequences."

Mansford stepped closer. "Are you saying it's too late?" He opened his coat, revealing his holsters. "I'm equipped," he said, "both physically and psychologically. My power may have diminished, but I've stroked the fires. I'm re-establishing the bond. It's working. I know it is. You know it is. Given time, I can do whatever's required."

"That's the problem," Surrogate explained, "there may not be enough time." He began to pace, then stopped, rolled his eyes and raised his hands. "I guess it's up to you, though. I can't begrudge you for trying, Michael Mansford. I only hope you can pull this off, that is, with all considering."

Surrogate's dubious stance infuriated Mansford, and he was about to express such when again, the entity crackled and vanished.

Mansford pounded fist into palm, but his frustration also propelled him to see things through. His mind raced. His eyes probed the room.

He spotted a small, sharp Punjabi dagger on the coffee table and without a second thought, inserted it into his empty holster, then reached into the closet, grabbed a couple of gray pallbearer gloves; donned them and felt more assured.

He moved toward the window, looked at the trees, the sky, pushed the pane upward, allowing a passing breeze to toss his cheek and once more, he sported the mask: its bolts and band now gone, the cool texture snuggling his features far better than before.

The distant buildings rushed through his expanding vision, through halls and walls, upstairs and downstairs, encircling him like a pumping carousel. Good, bad and otherwise, the faces held no meaning, streaming at such a velocity they blurred, made him dizzy.

He fell back, not knowing how to discern the phenomenon, then in defiance, pushed both his mind and body forth, through the window, rising high above the roof, scanning until he honed in on a familiar sight... Gyler, whose true self still oozed of deceit through his unassuming guise, his monstrous minions flooding the streets, mingling with the more susceptible passersby, who took their flyers and read.

The audacity of the scene shattered Mansford's mettle, diminishing his righteous rise, making him descend, swing back through the window, stumble like a rag doll across the carpet, onto the couch.

He grabbed the sides of his head…the divide between pearl and skin again indivisible…the mask suctioning tight, but then it let go, bouncing onto his lap. Tears streamed down his cheeks: a sure sign of defeat, but try as he may, he could not resign, not yet, anyway. He had to fight with all his might. He had no other choice. His town, his whole world, depended on it.

However, as the minutes passed and an uneasy calm fell over him, Mansford realized that though it was wise to move on matters, there was now a danger in doing so too fast. He had to rest, despite what Surrogate would say.

(XIX)

The phone rang with annoying persistence. He never wished to answer, but on those occasions he did, he spoke to the same people: Stark confirming the Gag Fest details, the mayor asking for advice on what he should say at the event…Clive suggesting ad designs.

There was no word from Murphy nor Standish. At one point, he had even asked Stark to visit her ravished home, if only to see if she had returned there, but of course, she had not. Through it all, the mask stayed close at his side, seeming to assure him that both parties were fine, neither sacrificed nor nibbled by beasts, but then this inference may have been but a handy contrivance to appease his general inactivity.

Day turned to night and night to day. He had a gala to attend, of course, but that did not mean he would abandon his specialized attire. He would take the mask, his handy holsters, his old gloves and dusty coat. He would let his charm do the rest.

It was about eleven of the next morning when he ventured out, looking spry in his black, three-piece suit and eclectic trimmings. He beamed an amiable countenance, waved at folks, shook more than a few hands when he made his way through the ceiling-fanned realm of Immaculate Banquet Hall, all the while ballyhooing what he promised would be a grand time for all.

He began to feel chipper, in fact, when he entered the kitchen area, where the caterers culled the ingredients for that afternoon's chicken cacciatore feast, and was happy as a lark to spot Father Bruno meandering along.

The priest's expression looked confident and wise. "So good to see you, Michael," he said, pulling Mansford close. "Thank you for inviting the children, my friend…and thanks as well for that lovely bicycle. Cindy was beyond thrilled when Mister Flynn delivered it. She's was so heartbroken when those ruffians stole her little, red one, you know."

"Well, I trust this one adequately compensates, Father."

"Indeed, it does. It's very stylish, such a striking green. I almost thought it was a boy's model at first glance, until I noticed the finer details." He smiled. "Now tell me, Michael, how did you know hers was stolen?"

"I'm in tune with the Lord," Mansford grinned and winked.

"Ah, you're always the joker, Michael, but then again, maybe you are—"

More people swept in, including Clive and Stark.

"My reporters are stationed out front," Clive said. "Even got some radio folks to record the required spiels. Should work well for ole' Percy."

"Thanks, Carl," Mansford said. "I appreciate the extra effort."

"Speaking of the mayor," Stark smiled upon sight of Mansford's new coat, "he's in the alcove, pacing up a storm. Could you help calm him down? He'll listen to you."

"Is it absolutely necessary?" Mansford asked. "There will be busses of kids here soon. I really should help Father Bruno with lining them up…as should you, considering we still have all those rats to distribute."

"Listen, Mike, if Percy steps out there and blabbers like a goon, you'll never forgive yourself. I'm not exaggerating. He's really that distraught."

"Very well." Mansford reminded himself that the gala's scheduling was to bolster the mayor's support. "I'll see what I can do."

They squeezed into a small, open room, just beyond the kitchen's view, where a short, bald, spectacled man in a fine spun suit sauntered to and fro, mumbling as a rubber hand ticked from the front of his neck.

"Mayor," called Stark, "Mayor…Mike's here."

"Oh, my," Poindexter ended his rumination, "yes, of course, Mike. How are you?" He yanked the hand loose, tossed it to the side and blushed. "It's so good to see you." He grabbed Mansford's hand and shook it. "Things have been moving so horribly fast these past few days. It's like I'm caught in a bad dream. I don't know which end is up."

"To say the least," Stark corroborated, "we got a real rabble rouser on our backs. That's why we pushed up the convention. It'll lessen the bastard's momentum."

"Amazingly, that's what he has," nodded Poindexter, "momentum and completely based on lies. I keep Brink Town's economy going, don't I, Mike? The various Mansford establishments are doing uncommonly well. Other businesses are flourishing, as well, despite the financial woes plaguing the rest of the country. I grew up around here, from very humble beginnings. I've never indulged in any shady deals, discouraged or alienated anyone, have I? Everything's on the level with me, I swear. I just can't imagine why anyone would say such things."

"I know," Mansford affirmed, "and you'll tell those gathered what you just told me. You'll push the truth, plain and simple, and we'll help it along with good-natured camaraderie. When the dust clears, folks will know that Percival Poindexter always has been...and staunchly remains...a man for the people." He crossed his heart. "I promise you that."

The mayor's eyes conveyed a sincere desire to believe, but Mansford knew the poor man's doubts were strong. Something had to be done...and fast.

Mansford placed his hands upon the mayor's shoulders, his fingertips tingling, his eyes blazing.

"What...what are you doing?" the mayor stammered. "Are you trying to hypnotize me? With all due respects, Mike, it won't work. Really, I'm not prone to—"

In a snap, Poindexter's jovial aura...as once witnessed in the wake of any number of uncontested elections and obligatory events...formed in both men's minds: carefree and well intended, one of the last of his kind in what was now an unethical scene. It was this unfettered guise, and this alone, that Poindexter needed to project and through the Persona's nurturing, it reared itself, wiping away any trepidation.

"Like I said," Poindexter chuckled, "I'm not prone to such pallor tricks. I appreciate the effort, Mike, but you're wasting your time."

Mansford lifted his fingers, lowered his gaze in feigned defeat. "I guess you're right, Percy. Well, you can't blame a guy for trying."

"Oh, not at all," Poindexter continued, looking for his novelty, which Stark snatched from the nearby table and tossed back. "For what it's worth, I do feel a trifle more at ease." He squeezed the hand below his chin and tested its pendulous swing. "If I can stay focused, say what I have to say, I might even have some fun with this."

"That's the spirit," said Stark. "Have fun. Let people know you're having fun, that you stem from the same fun-loving roots as them, and you do, Percy. You truly do." He nudged Mansford. "Oh, and don't forget to throw in a few good-natured knocks at your opponent. That's most important as well, right, Mike?"

"Ever so." Mansford seized the chance to slip away.

He strolled through the kitchen, into the banquet area, accepting wry compliments on his choice of attire, exchanging more smiles, shaking more hands (particularly those of reporters, equipped with either microphone or pen and pad), gazing through a front window as the first bus rolled in, the children leaping about inside, their little mouths jabbering, shouting.

Yep, thought Mansford, Ned's going to love this.

Mansford walked outside, noticing the Immaculate staff members alongside several stacks of boxes. The bus driver yelled at the children to settle down and to line up single-file, which led the first, a floppy capped teen with pugnacious nose, to burst forth.

"I wanna rat," he cried. "I heard they're givin' out rats."

A little girl in a disheveled dress followed. "Look...there they are in the boxes...see?"

"Yeah," the boy exclaimed, rubbing his hands. "Rubber Fright Rats it says...let's see what they look like."

A well-groomed, middle-age man in plaid attire, standing alongside the nearest stack, tried to ward the youngster off, stating, "Hold up there, son. You've got to line up first," but it was too late, for the youngster had rammed himself into the stack, knocking it over, causing a slew of the fabricated rodents...all adorned with their cute, crepe-paper GYLER'S A RAT kerchiefs...to cascade onto the lot, eliciting shrill shrieks as they bounced across the asphalt.

At this point, the other children dashed from the bus, feet kicking, fists flying, while Father Bruno and Stark made their way out, waving their arms and insisting they behave themselves.

More boxes fell. More workers reeled. More rats were squeezed. Girls squealed, their tiny voices intermingled with the spewing squeaks, while a few of the braver ones bunched a few by their springy tails and flung them into the boys' guffawing faces.

In the center of it all, the pug-nose boy grabbed as many of the rubber specimens as he could, ripping the crepe paper from off their necks as he squeezed, but Stark cut him off and smacked his hand.

"What's wrong with you, kid? Show some respect. We put those on there for a reason."

"Aw, stick it in your ear, Mister," the boy retorted flinging a rat into Stark's chest. "Ain't no rat gonna wear a sissy kerchief. It's stupid."

Stark's face turned red, and he lunged for the lad, who proceeded to bolt under his aggressor's legs, only to run straight into Father Bruno, who then chastised him.

Mansford moved onward, eyeing the many crepe denouncements that had landed on the ground. The summer wind ushered them along, up and over the flanking fences. He was confident they would reach those they were intended to offend.

As another bus entered, the little bicycle girl from his vision appeared at the first vehicle's door. With help from the driver, she guided her green Schwinn downward. She then hopped on it and wheeled past Mansford, clicking its handle bell, offering a gracious, unknowing nod: a sentimental enough gesture that should have warmed his heart, but instead instilled within him not only sobriety, but renewed urgency.

He wondered if the frivolous revelry acted as an intended reminder of how important it was to right wrongs, to make amends, and no more paramount an example was to find Murphy and Standish. He still believed their presence was near, so perhaps with further focus, he might yet accomplish the goal.

However, for the attempt to succeed, a number of things must occur: the first and most foremost was whether the mayor's performance could instill the required good cheer.

(XX)

After an arduous hour of scuffling and corralling, the children were seated, though demanding ice-cream and cake before the main course. They also squeezed their obstreperous rats at one another from across their tables, much to Father Bruno's befuddlement.

Mansford, Stark and Clive sat at the table closest the stage, where Poindexter and staff were also to sit. Sutton joined them, having arrived a short time prior, making it known he did not plan to stay for the entire span: just chat some, fill his belly and return to Blessed Tidings for some basic chores before dusk.

After a brief spell, one of Poindexter's older, surly-faced staff stepped on stage, positioning himself before a tall, thin microphone and requested that all stand for the Pledge of Allegiance, which even the rowdy children

She…wheeled past Mansford…

were honored to oblige. He then requested everyone be seated, looked down at the table and focused on Mansford and Stark, stating, "Welcome to the Annual Esoteric Incorporated Gag Festival, as established by Mister Michael Mansford and his diligent right-hand man and gala organizer, Mister Ned Stark. Mister Stark will present some of the latest Esoteric products to premiere this fall. As has been our tradition these past seven years, our Honorable Mayor, Mister Percival Poindexter is here to christen the ceremony with his presence, which will be followed by a luscious chicken-cacciatore meal, courteous of Collodi's Catering, located in scenic downtown Brink Town." He turned to the side, positioning his hands to clap. "Mister Mayor."

Applause, underscored by some dissonant whistling and squeaking, followed, and onto the stage, Poindexter shot, his right hand shielding his throat, but once he turned to the audience, he swung, churning a cacophony of laughter.

"Whoa, ho-ho," Poindexter guffawed, rocking his hips, making the clutching hand tick faster. "Look at me. Look at me." Flashbulbs popped. "It appears my would-be competitor, Ben Gyler, has me by the throat. Whoa, ho-ho."

More applause, chuckles and squeaks shook the hall, rattling the dishes, glasses and silverware. Stark glanced at his boss and winked, while Mansford's felt a tremble coming on, centering about his left hip. He realized the revelry was akin to a magical incantation, a prelude for some momentous occurrence yet to come.

Poindexter writhed a tad longer, then pulled the hand off him, throwing it upon the stage, where he pretended to stomp it, generating even greater, raucous fanfare and camera flashes, before kicking it onto the table, where it landed between Mansford and Stark, with the latter seizing it, holding it up and waving it in such a way to quell the uproar.

"Thank you. Thank you, ladies and gentlemen," Poindexter said, craning his neck back toward the mic. "It's sure a pleasure to see you all again, albeit with some short notice this time around, but considering I have a little fight on my hands...and evidently must devote more time to this year's campaign...I appreciate the unexpected indulgence and welcome you to another fun-filled Mansford-funded Gag Festival...one I'm confident will rival all others to date."

A polite, more subdued round of applause ensued.

"We're already off to a great start," the mayor continued. "Even our young guests are indulging in the fun with their oh-so-scary rats, I see."

The children giggled, a number of them hoisting and crunching their gifts.

"My, oh, my…horrid, little creatures, aren't they, kids?" the mayor said. "And what's that I saw wrapped around the creatures' stumpy, little necks?" He squinted, then shook his head. "Ah, yes, I should have known. It's the very name that's plastered all over town…that of the ever diligent man-of-the-people…my newfound adversary…Mister Ben Gyler."

A few boos and shrieks followed. Mansford remained focused despite the continued joviality, hinging on Poindexter's words, imagining he was controlling the mayor's verbiage, as might a ventriloquist, not that he by any means perceived the mayor a dummy. Quite contrary, for Poindexter's consciousness played with deft autonomy, and Mansford, abetted by his rising alter-ego, had the most at stake in such. After all, Poindexter's success would ensure his.

The mayor's eyes twinkled, absorbing the reporters' scribbling pens, their raised mics, knowing full well his words and actions were being recorded.

"My opponent claims to be a man of the people," he continued, "but a true man of the people wouldn't just pop out of the woodwork to publicize his presence. His existence would be known, just as mine is." He cupped his heart. "Now, sure, folks, I've attended many special affairs like this over the years, but so have you in the name of good fun, and like you, I work every day, albeit in a nice office in a place called City Hall, but never once have I forgotten my roots. I still frolic in them every day when I walk the streets, and you know my sincerity whenever we pass one another on the street, exchanging our humble hellos. Yessiree, no ifs, ands or buts about it, I'm one of you, and just like you, I enjoy my time most when it's spent with good friends, so let's get the festivities rolling, have ourselves a nice meal, engage in some humble conversation, and see what new wonders Esoteric Incorporated has sprung upon us for this year."

Then much to everyone's belly-groaning delight, he clapped and waved the waiters inward, leading the enticing scent of fresh salad and spinach soup to fill the hall.

As Poindexter descended the stage and made his way toward the table, Stark glanced at Mansford and said, "See? The son of a gun did good… short, sweet, and every note hit."

Mansford lifted the rubber hand and chuckled. "He also made good use of the prop. A shot or two will appear in tomorrow's edition, right, Carl?"

"Wouldn't have it any other way," said Clive and glanced over at the beaming mayor. "Nice job, Percy. You were a veritable Red Skelton."

"Gosh, I wouldn't go that far," the mayor said, "although I am quite the fan. I actually saw Skelton in Atlantic City last year. He's a bellyful of laughs. I'll tell you, that young man's going places."

"As are you, Mayor," said Mansford, "and your monologue seals that deal." He tossed Poindexter the hand, making the mayor roll his eyes and stash it onto his lap. "Now, don't be so fast to hide that. It might prove effective for upcoming gigs."

"Funny props have their limitations," Sutton grumbled. "Radio never does pantomime any justice." He glared at Clive. "You really gotta make sure, Mister Editor, that all the details are thoroughly conveyed on the printed page. I also think, for the remainder of the evening, the mayor should take it to the hilt." He shook his finger at Poindexter. "You still gotta interact with Stark, when he presents the rest of the gags. Throw in more political knocks. Keep it rolling. Don't let up."

"Yes, yes, of course." Poindexter looked to Stark for support. "We're going to ad-lib it, right?"

"Like I told you," said Stark, "just react to what I toss at you. It'll all fall into place from there, and this will ensure more photos for the paper. It's guaranteed."

As the men continued their constructive exchange, Mansford discerned a commotion in the distance. He turned, assuming it was only the children acting silly, but then noticed the pug-nose boy and a few others, pressing against the window. Curious, he excused himself and headed over.

"I'm tellin' ya," said the pug-nose boy, "I heard 'em all the way back at the table, croakin' like frogs."

"Ah, you're full of it," a pudgy boy in a snug-fitting, striped shirt said. "Where are they? I don't see nothin'?"

"They moved back into the trees," the pug-nose boy explained, "but I bet they're still out there, just hidin'. I'm tellin' yah, they got four arms, four legs, but changed back into men."

"Ah, it's probably just a gag," said the pudgy boy. "Ain't that the whole point of this shindig, anyway?"

The boys sensed Mansford's presence and darted back to their table, just as a flabbergasted Father Bruno leapt forth, shaking his fist at them.

Mansford, unable to restrain his concern, looked about and then crept out the door, into the twilight expanse, peering past the distant trees, a mere hop-and-a-skip from where the old Catholic church stood. He knew the boy had seen what he claimed. It was now a matter of whether the entities still remained in the vicinity.

A slight breeze stroked Mansford's face, and with it, came a startling stench, strong enough to eclipse even that of the cacciatore. After a few seconds, it faded, sweeping on to the trees, among which Mansford spotted several quickening shadows, whose attributes insinuated both man and beast.

He strutted back toward the hall, confident that they saw him, and for now that was enough to give him the burgeoning upper hand. He only had to wait, savor their growing despair, and if in panic, they dared try anything rash, he believed with every ounce of his conviction, the Persona could face them head-on.

●●●

The Great Beguiler bent down, and with his pale hand, picked up the slither of crepe paper that crossed his shoe. He held it toward the descending sun and unleashed a terse croak.

Among those gathered, whether disguised denizens or mere misguided mortals, a feeling of dread spread, but none was hit harder than Pickwick. He stepped forward and told his leader, "I didn't think they'd counter this fast, let alone use something as foolish as novelties."

"I find the proceedings most distasteful," said the Beguiler, "and I'm holding you responsible." He raised his hand, as if to strike. "I want this matter fixed immediately, my self-proclaimed high monarch."

Pickwick cringed, cleared his throat and assured him, "Yes, of course, consider it done. All I have to do is reschedule tomorrow's plans for tonight… stage it all right outside their sacred hall." He pointed to the facility. "The reporters are already there, and if we make enough commotion…"

The Beguiler grinned. "Fine…We shall steal the night from them, and claim tomorrow in the process." He crumbled the paper, tossed it at Pickwick's chest and fixed his extra set of eyes on the builidng. "From that point, there will be no turning back. Victory is ours."

(XXI)

Despite what he had detected, Mansford continued to enjoy the proceedings, even when the orphans engaged in a table-spanning food fight with ice-cream and cake. Of course, in the back of his mind, he realized a far greater distraction loomed. It was just a matter of how and when it unfolded.

"I'm heading out," said Sutton, finishing off a big chunk of chocolate cake. "I should get back to the cemetery before nightfall and keep an eye on things."

Mansford shot him a disapproving glance. "Trust me, Phil, you'd be better off here. If anything odd is bound to happen, it won't be far from where we're sitting." He raised his voice a notch, ensuring he was heard over Poindexter and Stark, who had since taken center stage, demonstrating some sound-effects handkerchiefs. "We'll need as many men as we can to keep the kids at bay, not that I think they'll be in harm's way by any means, but just the same…"

"Go on, go on," Stark urged Poindexter, prompting the mayor to rehash the effect. "Now, what's that sound like, your Honor? Go on…think about it."

Poindexter shrugged.

"Sounds like your opponent," Stark slapped his knee, pressing the bulbous cloth several more times. "Go on…give it a whirl. You emulate him perfectly."

Poindexter followed suit, igniting not only more laughter, but a cacophony of squeaks and a welcome barrage of furious flashes.

Clive, meanwhile, reached over, tapped Mansford hand. "Couldn't hope but overhear, Mike. Anticipating something bad?"

Poindexter's aide regarded them with evident concern, his ears bent to catch every word, but Mansford was quick to utter, "I don't anticipate anything we can't handle," and was content to leave it at that and then noticed the children again clustered at the window.

Mansford rose and hunkered his way toward them, his trail unnoticed due to Poindexter and Stark's shenanigans, and as he crept behind the children, he heard the pug-nose boy confirm, "I told you I saw 'em," to which his pudgy friend replied, "Big deal. They look like any other folks to me."

Mansford saw them lined beyond the far fence: row after row of the beady-eyed and bleary-eyed, depending upon their particular emanation. He also spotted the creature from Pickwick's kitchen, now much taller, with thick, curly hair, and at his side, the dwarf now appeared average in height and outside of a disproportionate arm and leg, rather sinewy.

"Get back to your table," Mansford ordered the children, and they snapped like a whip to their seats, again greeted by the ever exasperated priest.

"Keep them away from the window," Mansford told the father, cocking his thumb toward mounting mob, "and away from the door. It appears we have some opposition growing."

Mansford did not mean to be so blunt, but at this point, his emotions were shifting, his thoughts sharpening. His head spun. Stars formed before his eyes.

"Are you all right, Michael?" asked the father, noticing the odd way Mansford wavered.

"Yes, I'm fine, Father, fine, indeed."

However, his statement was only obligatory, for his attention was aimed more at why Poindexter and Stark's banter had skidded into confused whispers.

Clive and Sutton cut their way toward Mansford, moving to either side as he turned, gazing outside, while one-by-one the reporters began to flank them, anxious to document any potential trouble.

As Mansford anticipated, the mob moved several feet inward, with flannel-shirted Fred and Pete visible in the forefront, their eyes big and zombie-fied.

Pickwick and Pascale lumbered from out, hoisting a large crate, which they dropped not far from the lot's unfenced opening.

"Guess it's confrontation time," said Mansford, watching more members join the mob. He slipped on his gloves, then poised his hand above his left hip. "It's happening sooner than I thought."

However, just when he expected the King Guaner to waddle forth, a slender, fair-haired woman emerged.

"Glory be," gasped Sutton, "it's…it's Stacey!"

"Yeah," Clive acknowledge, "that pretty gal you brought by my office. I'd know her anywhere."

Mansford was too stunned to speak and absorbed her golden radiance. The final flickers of sunlight dashed off her brow, while her body stood in stiff, majestic contrast, adorned by an outdated, but no less elegant counterpart to Mansford's jacket: a black, silk Wickford blouse and long, snug matching skirt.

She stopped stiffly inches before the crate, allowing her father and Pascale to lift her onto it. She then promptly raised her arms, looking upward as if in prayer, invoking the image of Fritz Lang's fickle, cinematic "Metropolis" robotrix: by no means the innocent lady Mansford had so quickly come to adore, but rather an insidious, mind-altered variation.

By this time, through flawless sleight of hand, the mask was clasped to his face, its pearly constitution caressing his cheeks and brow, fluctuating in a symbolic nod to what transpired. He ascended like a ghost, gossamer and sheer, and those around him failed to detect his physiological change, unaware that he had seeped through the glass.

It was as though time had stood still, at least in Mansford's mind, as he, the Persona, devoured the words that passed the fair maiden's lips.

"My name is Stacy Standish," she declared, her voice strong and shrill, as if carried via some metaphysical means. "My step-father you've met, Jon Pickwick, museum curator, and like him, I am but one of Brink Town's many poor…poor not in monetary means, but poor in heart and soul."

The elocution was not Standish's, but rather the Beguiler's, who now used her as Mansford dared not to use Poindexter: a mouthing puppet.

Unsettled by the sight, the Persona spread his translucent arms, his coat expanding like dark wings.

"Yes, poor," she iterated, her stare searing through the Persona's fluctuating molecules, "poor in spirit, that is, when the majority dares to dictate one's beliefs. If I dare not believe in God, is that not my right? If I wish not to believe in such, is such also not my right?" Her face contorted into a compassionate grin. "Well, I believe the working class deserves a chance to believe as it desires, to have a stake in what this town makes. Why should I be deprived of that belief, when the opposition ridicules me, wants me to remain silent? I ask you, my fellow citizens, is such suppression the American way?"

Playing villainy as virtue…how clever, the Persona thought, and how persuasive, just like the misconstrued adage that prevailed overseas. Oh, how sad it was that people glazed over the truth and saw only what they wished to see.

"Our dear Mayor Poindexter hides inside," Standish continued, her arms pulling inward, "playing with toys that rich men will sell, earning immense capital that most of us might never hope to see." She pouted, her hands now clasped. "That's fine, I suppose, and some would argue that is as much the American way as the freedom of expression I advocate, but when such is done to mock those of opposing opinion…when it's done with sight gags and caricatures leashed by the name of a man whose inalienable right is to stand up and fight…then I, my good citizens, must differ."

The mob murmured, a few even croaked. This inspired the Persona to adapt a widening perspective, a portion of which remained on the hall: the mayor, now pressed against the window, trembling with burgeoning tears, while a handful of reporters shot beyond the threshold, drawn to the magnanimous display.

The Persona realized he had to penetrate Standish's mind, bring forth her true self, make her denounce the vile propaganda she blabbered, and perhaps with this, even those lined on the adversarial side, would have no choice but to embrace the truth.

"This is why I, an average, young resident," Standish shouted with passionate fury, "endorse Ben Gyler. I believe in his humility, his dedication to the common—"

The words became stuck in her throat. Her eyes watered, her misconstrued thoughts crumbled, as the Persona's auspicious aura infiltrated her thoughts with a face so ethereal and white that it washed over her soul.

Her contempt faded, but the Beguiler intervened, snatching the words, twisting them around to make her blurt, "Oh, enough of this charade. I can stand it no longer. We all know Ben Gyler is our man, but there's a far greater issue at hand…a need for spontaneous justice." She raised her fists, shook them and stiffened with impassioned conviction. "A police officer has been kidnapped…kidnapped by Poindexter's corporate posse. His name is Murphy…Jack Murphy, and he's been missing for nearly two days without consequence."

In that instance, the Persona's presence slipped away, the Beguiler's mental tendrils harnessing her consciousness to the point that she fainted into her father's arms. On this cue, the conniving puppeteer sprinted through the crowd and with a spirited leap, assumed her place upon the crate. With feigned sorrow, the phony looked down upon her, shook his head and to the reporters, pointed.

"Document this, my good men," he cried, the fluency of his improvised lie as smooth as silk. "The lady's right…this was never meant to be a mere campaign, and her little intro was but a prelude before the main rouse."

He sneered, gazing ahead, undaunted by the confronting apparition and with every ounce of his contempt, he immobilized the Persona, leaving him as if a ghost frozen in the air.

"Word about the street," Gyler shouted, "says the poor officer was seized because he had knowledge of embezzlement, of a purging of tax-payer funds…and yes, all within the deceitful confines of the Poindexter administrator. Officer Murphy even visited my campaign headquarters, shared his astonishing claim with me. Oh, how he feared for his very life because of it. I only wish I had placed more stock in his words, brought them into the light, for it did not take long for the political fiends to snatch him. Ask anyone who knows the man…has questioned why he's been uncharacteristically absent from his beat." He laughed, emitting a weird, nervous stench, which to those unknowing might have seemed origin-less. "I wouldn't put a pass if these pompous hooligans have him tied up in back, to mock him as they parade about, laughing, joking, finding yet another means to horde another unnecessary buck."

Though the Beguiler's words were too lofty to have come from a mere commoner, that did not stop them from resonating with those who heard them…inside or out. Even the Immaculate guests could not help but pause and wonder, and this riled the stationary Persona, and with every fiber of his ethereal being, he broke the invisible chains that bound him and forced his mind into the demon's.

The Beguiler writhed in pain and swayed upon the crate, while the vigil Pascale grabbed his legs, maintaining the veiled monster's vicarious position. The translucent Persona, however, wasted no time in slapping the creature off his perch and then pounded upon his obedient disciple, hurling him into the confused crowd, while keeping a keen eye on Pickwick, who stepped back, his daughter dangling in his arms.

A mad, emotional spree encompassed the scene, with children bursting from out the hall, screaming and yelling as they spilled onto the lot. Reporters and mayoral staff also lunged forth, with Gyler supporters meeting them head-on, and whether by accident or plan, punches were traded.

Mansford grew troubled by the ensuing struggle, causing the Persona's psyche to shake. His alter-ego bolted back, readapting physical form, leaving those gathered at the window with no reason to suspect he had left, let alone that he had secured his magical mask back into its compartment.

"Oh, my God," cried the ruddy-eyed Poindexter, "the children…oh, the poor children."

This prompted Mansford…despite his hindering cloak of mortality…to sprint from out the hall, into the sweltering melee, joining Father Bruno, who tugged along as many children as was he could, insisting they return to the hall, but by this time, it was apparent that the bulk of them were well immersed in the tumultuous mix.

"Butchy," the father hollered at the pug-nose boy, "get back here!" But the youngster scooted between a scrawny reporter and the towering dwarf and granted the latter a hard kick to the shin.

The diminutive entity's skin creased, and it reached down, revealing an extra pair of arms, but the boy leapt backward, stumbling into the reporter, who fell forward, atop the creature, which then scratched and clawed at the man, who proceeded to slap it in the head.

Mansford snatched the pug-nose boy and tossed him in the priest's direction. He then snatched his dagger, posing it for any Gauner to see and rounded the children back toward the entrance, leaving only the little girl on her Schwinn to wheel among of the gnashing, croaking brawlers.

"Come here, sweetie," he begged, the urge to reactivate the Persona surfacing strong, but not yet hitting its pinnacle. "Come here, before you get hurt."

The girl locked eyes with him and careened as one of the smaller imposters leapt up to kick at her bike: a cruel, craven stunt captured by a series of camera flashes.

It was Clive, in fact, who had triggered one of the cameras, which one of his employees had dropped in the midst of brawling. Its flash blinded the stubby Guaner, who scurried, aware that his actions had been captured. The elderly editor then snatched the child before she tumbled, tucking her under his arm, grabbing the bike by the handlebar.

"Got her, Mike," he cried, as the bewildered lass gawked at Mansford. "We've also got ourselves some nice, incriminating evidence. Wait till those shots show up in tomorrow's edition. Folks won't sympathize with anyone who'd harm a child. Our side's gonna look good…mighty good."

"Gotcha." Mansford returned his dagger to the makeshift pouch, while helping Father Bruno guide the remaining children inside.

A disheveled Sutton dashed over to Mansford, panting, "It's breaking up…see? The bastards are retreating."

Stark surfaced from the other side, spouting, "All right…terrific." He dusted himself off, blood curling down his nose. "We've still got ample casualties, but all in all, not bad for being outnumbered."

He was right about that, and the few folks left standing, mostly caterers and reporters, shrugged, egging on those who retreated to come back and fight. If only they knew the dangerous, inhuman attributes that many of their opponents harbored.

"Hey," said Sutton, "that's Fred over there…sprawled out on the ground. See him?"

"Yeah," Mansford acknowledged, "and Pete, just a few feet from him." He closed the door and stepped along the façade, taking a moment to glance through the window, reassured that Poindexter was assisting Father Bruno in reseating the garrulous children. "I actually spotted them earlier in the crowd, before Stacy showed up."

Fred and Pete's unconscious faces were positioned on their sides, bruised just as they had been that fateful night.

"Let's have a look," said Sutton, heading toward them, "but be careful. I'm telling you, there's always a catch to those two conniving clowns."

"Oh, I'd say they're relatively harmless at this point," said Mansford, as he and Stark followed, watching the rest of the rabble fade beyond the trees, along with another passing stench. "If anything, I'd say, they're light in the head, susceptible to any strong spell that might be cast their way."

"Same difference," Sutton growled. "Like I said; connivers."

They approached the men, Mansford kneeling next to Fred, and Sutton and Stark next to Pete. Mansford poked Fred's cheek. Sutton did the same to Pete. The battered men stirred and opened their eyes.

"What's…what's goin' on?" asked Fred.

"Yeah, where…where are we?" asked Pete.

"You were part of a goddamn rally," said Sutton. "It helped ruin Mike's Gag Fest. How's that for size?"

Pete sat up. "Rally? What the hell are you talking about, yah old coot?"

"That's right," said Fred, sitting up. "You play around too much. The Fest never happens in July." He then looked about and frowned. "Does it?"

"This year it does," said Sutton, "or at least, that is, it did."

At this point, Mansford felt aloof, with a new tingling rising from his hip to his arm, to his head, which conveyed in an alternate voice, *"Let's resume, old sport. Let me guide you, so that you may guide them."*

Upon this inner command, Mansford snapped his fingers, pulled Sutton and Stark to the side and whispered, "Let's get them out of here, to some place where they can adequately clear their heads. If we play our cards right, they might even lead us to the bad guys' hub…to Stacey… Officer Murphy."

"Sure," said Stark, "but what's a good place?" He paused. "Esoteric is winding down at this time of day."

"The night shift's there," said Mansford, "still enough folks to distract."

"Blessed Tidings would be good," suggested Sutton. "The work house is quiet."

"Too ominous," said Mansford, "too close to the cause." The tingling encircled his brow, forcing his eyes to widen, as the pages of Pickwick's text flashed throughout his subconscious, moving up and down, left to right and back again, before settling on a particular, translated track: "Guaners must deter the water, for such possesses the power to wash away their coveted, perspired grime and thus will weaken their senses. For this reason, those wise to this impediment have traditionally staked camp at the Rhine, but in fact, any river of any size can be made a temporary haven."

"Yes, of course," Mansford snapped his fingers, "why didn't I think of it sooner? We'll go to the Fishery. It's secluded, serene…for our purposes, environmentally sound." He glanced back at the hall. "I'd sure love to get this escapade settled. I'm afraid Clive can only push things in our favor so far. The word will spread about Murphy for sure, no matter what ends up in print."

"Come on," urged Stark. "It'll stay under wraps for a while. What's a few hours, a few days?"

"No," Mansford argued, "that's not Clive's style. He's a stand-up guy. He'll report what he sees fit and that means, just about all of it. Besides, the worse thing any of us can do is emulate the bad guys and distort the truth. We shouldn't forget ethics are essential to this cause."

He walked back to Fred, who was helping Pete to his feet and said, "We're going to get you guys out of here, give you time to rest…remember."

Fred winced. "I'm not so sure I want to remember."

"That goes double for me," echoed Pete, shivering as he kicked an abandoned rat, which bounced off into the distance with an annoying squeak.

"You don't have much of a choice, fellows," said Mansford. "In this instance, what you remember may very well decide our fates."

The men glanced at each other, but after a few seconds, nodded.

Stark also punctuated the matter with a solid clap. "Well, guess we might as well get going. It's probably better if we stick together. Besides, if I'm not mistaken, the Packard's rather roomy."

Mansford agreed, even though his thoughts bristled with renewed urgency and perhaps, a tinge of guilt. Indeed, Standish was very much alive…the intent to sacrifice her, though, null-and-void…but she was still out of reach, as was Murphy, wherever he might be, his unseen presence reduced to a damn, propaganda tool.

"*Despite all this,*" his inner-voice encouraged, "*you must keep the faith.*

Once we again form as one, we'll readily dispatch our adversaries, but we must tackle matters one step at a time."

Mansford remained stoic as he walked the group to the car, seeing no need to elaborate, only the impulse to engage in the next phase, and as they drove beyond the premises, a slow, steady burn engulfed both his body and mind, assuring him that, if only given a bit more time, he and his alter-ego could and would become fortified.

(XXII)

There was a foreboding feel about the dock as dusk died, but the splashing of the river proved soothing: perfect, Mansford thought, for a relaxed inquiry.

A couple old fishermen passed them, dragging their nets, smiling at Mansford in acknowledgement. He then led his friends on to the lime-shingled cannery.

"I've an office inside," Mansford said, opening the door. "It's in the back...nice and quiet, with ample chairs."

They followed him into the undecorated room. He made them coffee on an old, rusty stove, as they sat at an old, round table, trying hard to look noble and right, but their trepidation and doubt still prevailed. After all, they were in the midst of something indescribable, something they feared they may never understand.

Mansford placed a couple, chipped china cups in front of Fred and Pete, told them to "Relax...have a sip," then distributed cups to the rest, before circling back and forth, like a man deep in thought, or at the very least, on a mission for which he could not yet foresee an end.

"I don't remember much after they beat me up," said Pete. "I've some recollection of it, of you being there, Mister Mansford, but beyond that..."

"Yeah," added Fred, "it's all a big blur, "except for the voices. I think they planted whacky things in our heads, and of course, maybe did it all through some form of dark magic. Oh, yeah...strangest of all...there were all those crazy croaks."

"Croaks...yes," exclaimed Pete, "fast and urgent, but not so much like croaks, but maybe rather like some weird, ancient tongue."

"And there was that woman's voice," Fred continued. "I do remember that, mixing in with that quirky language. You remember it, Pete, don't you?"

Pete took a nervous sip, wiped his mouth and confirmed, "It was a female, all right, meaner than the men, meaner than the croaks, like she was maybe conducting the proceedings, using the others like pawns."

"What did these proceedings entail?" asked Mansford, tugging his gloved fingers as he paced, as if such might cull a more precise assessment.

"A plan," said Fred, "or at least that's what I'm assuming."

"An evil one, at that," said Pete. "It was though her words were an incantation: a mixing of English and that strange tongue, I'd say."

"Could you get any sense of the meaning?" Mansford asked.

The men looked at each other and laughed.

"Sure," Fred nodded. "She was playing the puppet master, and even in her own right, she was being played. I can't honestly say how I know that, but that's how it struck me."

"He's right," confirmed Pete. "That's the gist of it for sure."

Mansford grew rigid. "Was the young lady, Miss Standish, there?"

"I'm not sure," Fred answered. "Maybe."

"What of Jack Murphy?"

"I think he may have been," Pete offered, "at least at some point, anyway."

Sutton squirmed about his chair and pounded the table. "Make up your minds. Were they there or not? For cryin' out loud, you nit-wits."

Mansford raised his hand, signaling Sutton to hush. A tense silence followed.

"Gosh, it's hot in here," Fred blurted, wiping his brow. "Don't you think?"

Mansford nodded, walked to the window, opened it and for a few seconds, gazed upon the misty water, letting the fishy scent fill his nostrils. Pete sneezed.

"Bless you," said Stark.

"Thanks," said Pete, rubbing his eyes. "I must say, I feel kind of funny, kind of light-headed again."

"Now that you mention it," said Fred, "same here."

Little did they realize, Mansford had slipped into a trance, his gaze having become one with the river's flow, and as his stream of consciousness stretched, so did that of Fred and Pete.

"I recall," murmured Fred, "there also was a stench that rose among the words. It was worse than dead fish, or any earthly kind of foul scent. Frightening sounds surrounded it, like limbs stretching, bones snapping."

"The woman spoke of change," Pete blabbered. "Do you remember that?

She said no one would stay the same in body or mind, if the mission was to be achieved. Yes, I remember it clearly."

"So do I," gurgled Fred. "I remember how she said they were to change their plan to throw the other side off. She said that, because her daughter was originally intended as a sacrifice, she shouldn't remain one, that it might be more interesting if—"

The pause caused all to cringe in anticipation, except Mansford, but then for all intents and purposes, he was not Mansford at the moment he donned the mask.

"If what?" the Persona asked, his pearly lips fluctuating like a fine-tuned Disney cartoon.

"You...you know what," said Fred, as if channeling his own ghostly voice, only this one effeminate, "If she's not the one to be sacrificed, then we'll twist her mind, so that she'll sacrifice another. Her innocence will be lost...a tremendous gain to the Beguiler and his disciples. It'll be enough to shake matters up, give the cause the leverage to tear down the confines of order and stability."

"And who might their new sacrificial lamb be?" asked the Persona, though it was clear from his smug expression, the inquiry was rhetorical.

This time Pete answered: "The officer, of course, but for a brief while, his body will be kept nice and fresh. A thumb, toe or ear will end up at the station, perhaps even the Brink Town Times. Even if no one whispers a word, the receipt of such will be strong enough to generate immeasurable fear. Ultimately, suspicions will rise ever so high, and then—"

"I'd never permit that required time to ensue," said the Persona. "I'm far faster in my actions than any unearthly beast or for that matter, one of its mortal subordinates." His white lips curled at the ends, brushed by sinister pink. "Tell me, where is Murphy kept?"

Pete shivered, wanting to speak, but at this point, his mind grew so muddled, so layered and webbed that only scattered sounds and random images flashed within. The same also occurred to Fred.

"Try harder, gentlemen," the Persona requested. "I insist you give the matter all you can."

Though they wished to comply, they could only gnash their teeth, scratch at the table, knock over the cups.

Sutton and Stark, meanwhile, had also become absorbed in the kinetic hurly-burly, their minds swept by what Fred and Pete conjured: foul smells, burps and shrieks, limbs elongating, creaking while dark beasts writhed; bloody fluids splashed, circling around splintered boards, along dim walls,

"...I feel kind of funny...lightheaded..."

where chipped crucifixes and dusty Blessed Mothers appeared...then the hint of Murphy huddled in a corner, bug-eyed, his mouth gagged...but where, oh where, was this horrid place? Was it new, old, sacred or profane?

"Tell me, gentlemen, tell me," the Persona insisted, widening his arms and hovering, his coat flapping from the spiritual fervor he unleashed. "Where is this place?"

The quartet screamed in agony, unable to see, hear or share anymore, their heads hitting hard onto the table.

The Persona touched the floor. The wind doused, and in a snap, the mask was again secured at his hip.

Mansford cleared his throat and regarded his unconscious companions, the realization of their dismal state prompting him to wail, "Fred...Pete... dear Lord, are you all right? Ned...Phil...please, fellows, wake up."

After a moment, they raised their heads. Sutton and Stark regarded Mansford with tremulous admiration, as Fred and Pete pouted and sighed. Mansford, in turn, grabbed the coffee pot, again made the rounds, apologizing for any mental intrusion, explaining, "It's just part of the process, guys, the way it has to be until we get things ironed out. You understand, right?"

"Sure," said Sutton.

"Absolutely, said Stark.

Fred and Pete nodded, but looked dejected, wondering if the Persona might yet probe their minds, but Mansford had no immediate impulse. Whatever he had conjured and defined would have to work for now. He also realized the best way to cultivate such was through reflective solitude.

"Give me a moment," he said. "I'm going outside. I won't be long."

He sauntered into the river-tinged air, his heels clicking upon the dock, like some manic march, again catching the mesmerizing flow, recalling the elusive sensations he had gathered, praying he might connect to each scattered clue, when...

"Hello, my friend," Surrogate said. "My, what an impressive performance you gave."

Mansford saw the spectral shape a few feet behind, arms folded across his chest, his hazy face blurred in the nocturnal gleam.

"I'm glad you approve," Mansford quipped. "So, am I to assume you saw what I saw, and if so, what does it convey?"

Surrogate raised a finger, shook it. "Now, now, it's your job to solve that. The process won't succeed otherwise." He moved closer. "You very well know that. Virtue and piety will never stem from out the human condition if abetted with ease. What then would be the point of the fight?"

Mansford sneered. "Unfortunately, it's that type of ambiguity that makes me wonder, Mister Surrogate, if you're friend or foe?"

Surrogate shook his head. "You know I'm on your side, and I'm pleased by the way you're getting your house in order. After all, your little, lustful plunge could have permanently sidetracked this scene. Nonetheless, now with the variables neatly rearranged, you must beat these fiends at their own game; devise a new plan to rival their own." He pointed to Mansford's brow. "You've certainly accumulated enough ammunition, though in truth, you've really possessed it all along."

Mansford sighed at continued ambiguity. "Meaning?"

"As I've more than implied, even before your alter-ego rose, you harbored the acute ability to distinguish good from bad. Such opposite concepts sometimes ironically coincide, as you've witnessed, but you're not one so easily fooled. The greater of the two extremes always holds the higher ground, and only at such a vantage will you find it." He winked. "Again, you know this, of course, and that you'll only need to scan your basic surroundings to make the pieces fit."

Surrogate's riddling further infuriated Mansford, and in exasperation he was about to demand a succinct explanation when, as only expected, the specter crackled away, leaving only a funneling wind in his wake.

Mansford shook his fist: a pathetic reflex, at best. After all, he did realize Surrogate's intentions were sincere, and as daunting as it was to expand his faculties yet another stretch, he was confident he could succeed; but such would require a set-up even more specialized than the river.

He had to share his intent with the others, and so back to the cannery he dashed, where he relayed his need for additional adjustments.

"I understand if you need more time to yourself," said Stark, "but where's that leave us?"

"Don't fret," said Mansford. "I'll be happy to drive you back to Immaculate."

Sutton snickered. "Along with these two jugheads? What if they get riled, want to scoot back to those fanatics, tell them how you extracted certain info from them? Who knows? Maybe that's been the plan all along."

"I assure you," said Pete, "that's not the case."

"Correct," added Fred. "Whatever hold they had on us is most assuredly dead."

Mansford scrutinized the weary glint in their gazes, but try as he may; he lacked the confidence to chance their claims.

"Sorry, fellows," he confessed, "but to be on the safe side, it's best you stay here for the night." He turned to Sutton. "Phil, be a sport and keep an eye on them, will you?"

Sutton looked down at the table and hissed, "Yeah, sure, Mike, why not?"

"Thanks, Phil," Mansford then turned to Stark. "I'll get you back to the hall. You can help the folks clean up, also touch base with Carl and see what he might insert in the morning edition. You can head home from there."

"Aye aye, Admiral," Stark leaped up with an assured click of his heels. "I'm game."

With this affirmation, Mansford led his friend into the expanding dark. Both were weary and bedazzled, uncertain what might next come their way, but not afraid to face it.

(XXIII)

Stark asked Mansford at least a dozen questions in the time they reached the hall, but to each query, there was not much upon which the entrepreneur elaborated. In many respects, he was as baffled by how he had become enlisted in such a remarkable crusade and exceeded little beyond several rehashes of that fateful night when he had encountered the beguiling beast.

"Does Carl know all this?" Stark asked as they rolled into the lot. "I realize it's too crazy to put in print, but at the same time…"

"Carl's a professional," said Mansford. "He won't print anything he can't substantiate, so don't fill his head with any distractions. He senses the gravity of the situation just like rest of us. Let him do his job, stick to the facts as he knows them. Really, that's all we can ask, and, Ned, don't worry. I'll touch base by morn."

Stark got out, continuing on without looking back. Mansford watched him a brief while, before letting his eyes shift to the side, acknowledging the buses, their large headlights beaming, children poised near the glass… the pug-nose boy, his pudgy pal, the Schwinn girl, among others…still waving their rubber rats, their young eyes glistening as much of intuition as innocence, but it was the latter he savored, wishing he could make it his own.

The buses rumbled onward, Father Bruno standing at the rear window of the first, shoulders slumped, face drawn, still respectful enough to offer an affable salute when he spotted the Packard: a most poignant moment, despite its brevity, for it confirmed there was nothing sadder than innocence lost, from either sight or mind, and perhaps in that, mused Mansford, a most significant lesson had been learned.

He considered the matter for a long while, glancing again at the hall, watching the silhouettes moving within. He felt guilty for not lending a hand, but his conscience reminded him that rumination was the best way he could serve the citizens of Brink Town. It was just a matter of where to go.

As such, he decided to leave the lot and trekked for a spell in manic circles, his gaze bouncing, trying to nail the right place, the right feel for where he should be. However, the more he traveled, the harder it became to decide, and in little time, he found himself lost, not so much in location, but rather in thought.

On occasion, he would graze his hip, hoping the mask might ignite some much needed inspiration, but to initiate such, he still had to relax: a hard task in wake of his increasing agitation.

He meandered back home, but in seeing Charlie milling inside, decided to remain in his car and closed his eyes.

As sleep overcame him, his head slid onto the passenger seat, and before long, he dreamt of dark beasts and inhaled despicable stenches, but through it all, found no meaning, no cause, until he recalled Standish's virginal face, stalwart and undefiled. If only he had been a stronger man, harnessed his urges, given the matter more time to mature, he could have left her unmarred. If only there was someway he could reverse the process, take it all back.

Night progressed into morning, and the next thing Mansford knew, the sun was kissing his brow.

He sat up, his face drenched in cold sweat. He was ashamed for having lost so much time and again feared he had granted the enemy another advantage.

Disgruntled, he dashed from the car, into the building, just as Charlie was leaving, lunchbox in hand.

"Hey, there, Mister Mansford. Burning the midnight oil, eh?"

"Yeah, you might say that, Charlie. Say, did the morning paper arrive?"

"Sure did. There's a copy on the desk. It's a shame those bums ruined things for you. Heard the same crew was here yesterday." He pressed the box against his chest and drummed it. "I'll tell you, Mister Mansford, if they had shown up on my shift…"

Mansford ignored his boast and headed straight to the desk and read the headline: POINDEXTER'S PROTESTORS PUT ORPHANS IN PERIL.

"Now, that's an apt spin." Mansford was a trifle relieved, his eyes falling upon a fuzzy photo of the disguised Guaner, whose fake foot stretched toward the cycling girl.

"Horrible stuff for sure," Charlie continued, who had followed him back in. "Read the whole thing from front to back. Lot in there, you know. I even caught a blurb about it on the radio. There's been mention of a blonde, you might know. Now, she's not the one you brought by, is she? I only ask because the description sure sounds a lot like…"

"No…of course not," Mansford lied, considering the poor girl's actions had been forced. He then let his eyes scan an overview of the Gyler's entourage, including mention of the alluring blonde who spoke, but Clive's attribution was nameless and rudimentary enough to fit any number of females.

"Glad to hear that," said Charlie with an apologetic chuckle. "The young lady who visited here seemed like a nice girl, though too bad about the cop, huh? Don't know Murphy personally, but I've seen him around town. Always struck me as a decent guy."

"Trust me," Mansford was wrought with guilt, "he is, and that's precisely why these anti-Poindexter creeps nabbed him."

"So, you think it's them? That it's all part of the same sneaky stunt?"

Mansford smiled, knowing full well that Charlie would carry the word. "Yes, a stunt, evidently. You know as well as I, the mayor would never initiate such a despicable plan. His so-called competitor, on the other hand…"

"Sure, sure," Charlie embraced the notion. "It's really not so far-fetched, either, especially if the guy would be so inclined to put orphans in peril. If there's one thing I can't stand, it's those who stomp on the innocent for personal gain. It's just like what they're doing in Germany now, you know."

There was something in Charlie's off-the-cuff denouncement that helped Mansford summon that mystical surge he so craved. His body pulsated. His eyes glazed.

"You okay, Mister Mansford?"

"Yeah," Mansford muttered, as images of the rambunctious orphans danced through his head. He also recalled the Christian paraphernalia from his vision, heard the bones snapping, smelled the metabolic stench. "I was just thinking."

"Thinking." Charlie's tone was cautious. "About what, sir?"

"That I'm glad I talked to you, Charlie. You've actually opened my eyes to a few things."

"Well, it's my pleasure, Mister Mansford. Glad to be of service. I always try to look at things from a variety of angles. It's always been my conversational style, ever since I was a kid."

Mansford reached for the desk's farther end. "I'm going to use the main line, if you don't mind."

"Uh, don't mind at all, sir. Heck, this is your establishment, after all. You do as you please. Anyhow, like I was saying, I've always had the gift of gab…"

Mansford let him drone on, as he grabbed the phone, dialed Clive's number, but there was no answer, and why would there be? The poor man had been up all night, preparing the story.

"Yep, I could always leap from subject-to-subject," Charlie went on, "never afraid to speak my mind."

Mansford hung up, then dialed Stark, but again, no answer. He also tried Sutton, both at home and at the cannery, but in each instance, to no avail.

"Uh, having some trouble reaching folks, Mister Mansford?"

Mansford sighed, but in the solemn moment, conjured another idea. "Say, Charlie, could you do me a favor?"

"Favor? Why sure, Mister Mansford. Be most obliged."

"I'd like you to round up the troops," said Mansford, "at least before you get too tuckered out. Tell people what you know. Don't get into any scuffles, mind you, but to those you trust, those who'd be willing to pass along the good word; give them a decent earful, and if you see any of my friends…particularly Mister Stark and Mister Clive, even Mister Sutton, if by chance…tell them I'll touch base as soon as I can."

"Consider it done," said Charlie, swinging the box. "Always like chatting with Mister Stark. Can't say I've ever had the chance to chew the fat with Mister Clive, though, but I'd sure like to, and as for Mister Sutton, well, he's is rather on the grouchy side, but…"

"Please," Mansford interjected, "just let them know we need to catch up. That's all I ask, Charlie."

Charlie nodded, his expression now mirroring Mansford's solemn tone.

He patted Charlie on the back, then shot for the entrance, his feet gliding as if via mercury, smooth and fluid, his focus sharpening, expanding.

He knew where he had to go, what he sought. The question was: would it be, as he hoped, still there for him to find?

(XXIV)

Mansford knocked hard on the old, arched door.

"Coming, coming," said Father Bruno, shuffling nearer. "Give me a moment, please." He cracked the door, squinted into the sun, forcing his gaze upon Mansford. "Michael," he exclaimed. "Well, I'll be..." He opened the door wider, revealing his brown, moth-ridden smock. "What an exasperating time we had yesterday. I truly apologize for the children misbehaving." He gestured Mansford inside. "I've a hunch you've gotten no sleep, you poor man. Please, come in. I'll make some coffee, or would you prefer tea?"

"At this point, Father, neither," Mansford entered the humble, candle-lit abode. "There's something, though, I must ask of you."

The priest's eyes bulged, and he looked rather enchanted within the amber light. "Yes, Michael?"

"You have a storage area on the premises, don't you?"

"Why, yes, we do have such...a basic, storage cellar, if you will. It's right next door, under the children's church." The father tightened his flimsy cloth belt, studying Mansford's urgent expression. "I'll show you, if you'd like."

"Yes, please," said Mansford, and the priest wasted no time to sprint ahead of him, waving him onward, across the dewy grass, toward the adjacent chapel, its arched, stained-glass windows shimmering with a storybook aura best suited for kids.

"We go to the right," Father Bruno scooted beyond a cluster of little pews, "and head all the way to the back, past the pulpit. Behind the curtains, there's a trap door and stairs leading down to it."

Mansford stuck close to the father, watching as he clicked a switch on the planked side wall and knelt next to a dusty floor panel, which he removed via an old rusty hinge.

A putrid gust rose. The father winced, coughed. "Holy Mother," he stammered, pinching his nose. "What in the world?"

Mansford looked down into the dim, dank expanse, unsettled by the stench, but held his ground.

"Yep," he said, "they were here, all right."

"Good gracious," choked the father. "You mean...?"

Mansford stepped around him, dipping the tip of his shoe into the pit. "Yes, Father, the bad guys."

Father Bruno grabbed Mansford's leg. "You shouldn't go down there, son. Who knows what…?"

"It's all right, Father. I don't sense they're here presently. I just need to have a look."

The priest let go. "All right, Michael. Do what you must."

Mansford descended, his mind elevating, his entire body sparking like an electrical grid, as he absorbed not only the cellar, but also Father Bruno's vantage: an extra set of eyes to behold the sloppy, globed circle upon the concrete-cracked floor, the old crucifixes and statues, unfastened rope, a balled rag…long, tangled strips of masking tape.

"They had him here," said Mansford, as the priest followed behind. "There's no doubt of that."

"Who?" Father Bruno touched the cold concrete, tiptoeing around the muck, oblivious to the inadvertent extension of his invaded perception.

"Officer Murphy," Mansford replied. "They had him restrained here and," he continued with immense distaste, "they summoned more of their ghastly legion." He pointed to the shadowed inner circle, where large chunks of concrete were strewn and the dirt appeared clawed and tunneled.

"You mean, they came up from the ground? Oh, my boy, you can't be serious. There's no way."

Mansford lowered his head, and with rapid sleight of hand, placed the mask to his face, and along with it, the men's combined intuition heightened, as did a new flow of imagery.

There was Murphy, centered in the smelly sphere, bond and gagged; small, multi-armed creatures nearby, ramming upward and out, with the robed, hooded conductors skipping about, waving their hands at the monstrous procession; while in the backdrop, shivering and looking away, was the robed Standish and next to her, grasping her delicate arm, another slender figure, whose hooded brow obscured her face, but whose curly gray hair yet protruded; a woman the frightened young lady knew all too well.

"It's her mother," Father Bruno exclaimed and then added, "Marjorie… yes, Marjorie is her name." In catching himself, his projected view faded, leading him to turn to his friend and say, "Sorry…don't know what came over me there, Michael."

The Persona turned, causing the priest to shutter.

"You had a spurt of supernatural insight," explained the Persona, his once pearly sheen now resembling powdered flesh, his lips curling, though exuding no vile intent. "It generally happens when I'm awakened, when individuals are stationed near me, especially if they are ones Mansford trusts. In such instances, it's easy to share thoughts."

"I…I understand," said Father Bruno. "I feel rather foolish, though, considering all of this transpired under my nose." He frowned, as if about to beg for forgiveness. "I now realize they were here before the protest yesterday evening, plotting all along, conjuring their little demons, and that poor officer…oh, if I had only been more observant, I could have intervened, at least called the precinct." He rubbed his nose, gagged back a cough. "I wonder why they chose here to hide, when there were so many more viable places."

"These fiends take delight in defiling the sacred," the Persona elaborated. "What more precious a hideout than a church designed to enlighten children?" His eyes twinkled, and a spark of the regular, old Mansford insinuated itself. "Besides, you were far too occupied with getting the children ready for the gala. Why inspect every speck of every building, especially a musty, old cellar?" His voice then resumed its ethereal reverberation. "Now the question is, where have they moved on to, what next will they deem virtuous enough to besmirch?"

The father shrugged. "I wish I only knew."

The Persona looked upward, his facial lines deepening, his pupils sharpening.

"They're moving fast," he murmured, "keeping the Beguiler in constant flux, so he can grow as I'm growing without interruption, his mind expanding, his powers amplifying." The Persona rolled his eyes down at the priest, his countenance turning grave, angry. "I must go. I must catch up."

Father Bruno quaked, sensing the entity's urgency. "I know you're weary, Father," the Persona readapted Mansford's humility, "but if you could do me a favor?"

"Yes," the priest pledged, "anything."

"Spread the good word, my friend…spread it to all who'll hear. Tell them what you saw last night, what danger Poindexter's opposition has set forth. To those who dare doubt, remind them of all things gracious and pure, of how the other side will strip such away through lies and deceit. Convince them, Father, to embrace the self-evident truths within their hearts and above all, to keep the faith."

Tears filled Father Bruno's eyes. "Yes…yes, I can do that. Yes…I will do that."

The Persona smiled, and without further ado ascended, his coat flapping like angle wings, catapulting him from out of the doleful chamber.

The father followed, leaping past the curtain and saw that, beyond the pews, the church doors were flung open. He ran to the threshold, a gust smacking his cheeks, and in the distant sky, the pinprick of a coated figure buzzing, then fading from sight.

For a moment, the father's sight blurred, as did his mind, and up through his pores, a smoky, twinkling aura took form.

"Very well, my dear Michael Mansford," he said, from out the body he had dared occupy. "You're finally on your way." Beyond the gate, into the horizon, he then peered, absorbing the passing cars, the bustling people and declared, "And so now, will I…"

Father Bruno then blinked, touched his face…again smooth, fleshy… and though for a moment, he wondered what had come over him, he dismissed it, beelining back to his abode, determined to spread the word.

(XXV)

In and out, up and down, Brink Town fluctuated. Even for the Persona, the gamut of its calamitous sights and sounds proved exhausting.

Nevertheless, goodness…the pure, sweet, uplifting ideal of it… remained concealed among the many petty contrivances of its citizens: people short-changing bellhops, crooks hot-wiring cars, couples sneaking off on adulterous binges, dispirited grouches kicking puppies…It was, alas, all part of the varied human condition and with so many of its foibles bouncing about, to pinpoint any anchored amount of decency seemed daunting and frustrating.

He thought, perhaps, it best to catch only the bad scents, to unravel their origins and move on from there, but in the midst of the town's random fumes, such was difficult, until a puff of demonic perspiration cut front-center, and upon this, the Persona hinged his psyche.

Indeed, they were moving Gyler around, from vehicle to vehicle, street to street, building to building, surrounding him with both man and monster, shielding his presence, so that his mind might more better expand, allowing his odious clan to hid their plans, but with each hustling twist and turn, the Persona managed to discern the underbelly of their intent and the misfortunate souls linked to it.

He saw Murphy, still bound and gagged, eyes closed, his cheeks sweat-drenched as he was carted through endless dark chambers, his nose twitching, fighting off the disgusting odor, clinging to the sparse reprieve of Standish's perfume, but though fetching was her scent, could she be trusted?

The Persona allowed her face to fill his mind, like a blistering sun stationed at the center of the universe, bright white and golden fringed. However, despite her angelic blaze, he also sensed her lost innocence: the result of his mortal counterpart's selfish deed. What a pity, for she was now more susceptible to the Beguiler's hypnotic trickery, but as misguided as she was, would she actually follow through with the sect's insidious plan? Would she...when they so requested it...kill?

Questions...far too many questions. Far too many doubts...but the Persona knew that if he...if any who fought on the side of good...had any chance of winning this battle, optimism remained an irreversible course.

Standish's magnetic face faded like a dying sun, which in turn became deep blue, the hue stretching over the hurried people, revealing the ever tireless night guard and priest, on opposite sides of the town equation, buzzing with equal vigor to anyone willing to listen or debate, their arms animated, their mouths chattering in evident opposition to the Guaner cause.

Familiar faces emerged, yawning, rubbing eyes, forcing themselves into disheveled wakefulness, into their cars, zooming onto the streets: Clive passing the father; Stark approaching Charlie, information exchanged, concerns mounting, an innate understanding established, for they looked into the sky, perhaps without understanding why, only knowing that someone watched them, someone who cared, who knew, whose spirit grew, with a stalwart purpose to make things right.

The Persona descended, swaying like a feather, rocked by the insightful wind, his stare skimming the orphanage, the little church, onto the adjacent street, past the Packard's roof.

His feet touched the concrete. The mask found its way back onto his belt. He exhaled, inhaled until the confined, human side of him reformed... and a squeal of wheels squashed his meditative mood. It was only a truck, heading off into the distance, of no great consequence...or so he thought.

He pulled his keys from his pants and slipped inside the car, revved the engine, clicked on the radio and listened to the newscaster: "...a disturbance last night at the Immaculate Conception Hall, where mayoral hopeful Ben Gyler and supporters disrupted the annual Esoteric Incorporated Gag Festival with protests and brawls, in an attempt to challenge Mayor Percival Poindexter's bid for a third term."

He hung on every word as he was about to pull onto the street, but when he glanced up; he spotted a small, portly nun dashing from out the main entrance, her face wrought with panic.

He turned off the engine, leapt out to see what was wrong.

"Help, help," she hollered, her eyes darting in his direction. "Did you see? Did you…?"

Mansford skipped toward her, meeting her at the fence.

"Two men," she exclaimed, "they…they took the children…two boys, two girls. They put them in that old truck. Oh, you must have seen what they did…seen them head off."

"Sorry, Sister," Mansford cupped her tiny knuckles, "but I missed it. I'm certainly willing to help, though. If you could just tell me."

"But the truck was parked right in front of you. You must have seen it."

"Yes, I did see a truck, but I certainly didn't deduct—"

"We have to call the police," the nun said. "If only Father Bruno were here." She looked about. "I haven't seen hide or hair of him all day. I do hope he's okay." She gazed at the sky. "Oh, Lord, what are we to do?"

One of the younger nuns scuttled from the doorway, mouthing "I called."

Mansford relayed this to the trembling sister and guided her against the fence, assuring her everything would be all right, but at this point, he was uncertain, and it was then that his head began to throb with new images ushering through:

He saw the museum, the library, too…two purposeful bases bouncing to and fro, overlapping, separating, only to overlap again, but for what reason? Beyond the obvious fact that the Beguiler's subordinates worked at both stations, what was the meaning?

"*No need to look so hard,*" his inner voice said. "*As in the case prior, the connection lies beneath.*"

Mansford regarded the criss-crossing roofs and peeled away each surface, his gaze falling upon rows of books, artifacts, shelf after shelf oozing of insight, history, knowledge and the latter, he certainly knew, was such a sacred thing.

A stinging stench filled his nostrils: a hint of sweat and flame. He saw knives raised, heard gut-wrenching grunts and blood-curdling screams. It was more obvious than ever what the fiends were doing.

"They'll slaughter their lambs," he seethed, "and burn it all down, as if to pretend none of it ever existed. They'll then take their horrid crusade to the streets, march their trickery from city to city until nothing of value stands." His eyes grew teary, his words frigid. "It'll grow like Red Russia, Fascist Germany...Imperial Japan, but this time right in our own back yards, all without structure, without consequence, fueled by random impulse, torture and pain."

Mansford looked up; saw the elderly nun staring at him, her face taut and cautious, the younger alongside her, equally unnerved.

"I...I apologize, Sisters," Mansford stuttered. "I was just trying to gather my thoughts, to make sense of things."

Police cars peeled into the scene, leaving Mansford to wonder how much time had lapsed. He stepped back, leaving two spry officers to approach.

"What happened, sisters?" one asked.

"Two men entered the main hall," the elder explained. "They looked rough, with puffy faces, the way boxers do. They approached the children... the orphans, that is. We often tend to the surplus of children at this hour, you know...a few of older ones, mainly. Anyway, I asked the men what they wanted, but they pushed me back. Each grabbed a couple children... tucked them right under their arms...then strutted out of the building. Oh, how the youngsters struggled, especially the two boys...bigger, older, they are, you see...but the men had no trouble with them. It was as if they were robots...so rigid and expressionless."

"Did you notice the make of vehicle?" asked the other officer.

"It's was a truck," said the nun. "They threw the children in the back. One squeezed in with them. I saw it distinctly."

"Truck, you say?" said the officer, pulling out his pencil and pad.

"It was green," said the nun. "It was green, and on the side door, it said... Blessed Tidings Cemetery."

"Yes," the younger nun confirmed. "It did say Blessed Tidings. I saw from the window."

With a heavy heart, Mansford knew who the culprits were, and now feared for Sutton's welfare.

He tried to re-conjure his alter-ego, hoping to achieve its fullest formation, but realized the Persona still required time to re-cultivate.

"For now," his secret side advised, *"you enact your gentle foil. When the time comes, we will merge as one, with the Persona stronger, wiser than before, but for now, Michael Mansford, follow your instincts, assume your rightful role, and be assured, all will fall into place."*

Without further ado, Mansford leapt into his car, catching the cops' suspicious eyes as he pulled away, but he did not care. He was concerned only in returning to the river.

(XXVI)

Mansford pushed past the exiting cannery workers, swung open his office door and sighed.

Sutton was there and worse for wear.

"So much for being out of the enemy's reach," he snorted, wobbling in his chair as blood trickled from his mouth, a few chewed strings pasted to his bottom lip. "Really thrilled getting tied up like this, Mike, and in a veritable heat box no less. No one checked on me, thank you very much. Finally had no choice but to chew through the gag, and when I tried to yell, my throat was too damn horse to make a sound." Mansford yanked the string from Sutton's wrists and he raised them, exposing their raw indentations. "Ah…feels good."

"I am sorry about this. I'd have checked, except that I've been in kind of celestial limbo. I should have listened to you, my friend." He patted Sutton's shoulder. "So, when did the boys pull their stunt?"

"Not long after you left," Sutton answered. "For a while, they were chatting up a storm, like they didn't have a care in the world, but when they started to speculate on their circumstance, that's when their eyes got real glassy. I should have whacked them over their damn heads right on the spot, but instead," he tapped his temple, revealing a big bruise, "Pete hit me with the friggin' kettle, and Fred slugged me in the jaw. Then they had to go and close the window. Real considerate."

Mansford paused, as a spurt of text burped into his mind: "Though Guaners have an aversion to water, their human subordinates can act as liaisons, if the applied method of mind-control has been firmly stationed;and if the mental link has fallen dormant, such can be reactivated in the subjects per any Great Guaner's bidding."

"By chance, did the fellows say where they were going, Phil, what they were intending to do?"

Sutton brushed himself off. "Course not. I was just happy the goofs didn't kill me. Still, it was obvious they weren't working off their own

Mansford leapt into his car…pulled away…

accord. For what it's worth, you might want keep your mystical facade on constant alert. Something's on to us, and Fred and Pete only confirm it."

"Believe me," Mansford said under his breath, "that's not the half of it."

Sutton shot him an odd glance, then complained how he needed something to eat, had to wash up, call his wife and needed a ride back to the Immaculate, if only to get his pick-up. Yes, his pick-up, of course.

Mansford turned his ear from the river, listened to the sounds of the distant town: horns beeping, engines chucking…people conversing.

The latter sound grew more succinct, but why? Voices certainly did not travel in such a way.

Mansford also detected movement from afar: zigzagging motions through the alleys, a shuffling across sidewalks and streets, people flooding past one another, searching, but for what…for whom?

At closer range, Mansford sensed the passing dock workers, mingling with nearby residents, as they merged across the asphalt. The massive, ant-like procession astounded him, and it continued to grow, becomeing more imminent with each inch gained.

"What in Heaven's name?" asked Sutton, as he followed Mansford onto the dock. "What an odd sight. I sure hope it isn't the makings of another riot."

From the outer cusp of the crowd, Stark then appeared.

"Mike," he called, pushing his way through. "Phil…you guys see me? I'm over here. Here…see?"

There he was all right, disheveled but staunch, appearing as amazed as they were by the great congregation.

"I don't think these folks propose a problem," Mansford deducted, standing on his toes, waving Stark over.

"Maybe not," Sutton said, "but I still don't get it. What's happening? What's the point?"

Mansford could not offer an immediate answer, nor did he desire one, being both curious and pleased by the continuing spread of faces.

"Look there…hoisted upon those men's shoulders," he pointed. "It's Carl."

Sutton spotted Clive's ruddy face, elevated upon a couple of jockish men's shoulders.

"I'll be damned if it isn't…"

Mansford suckled the fluctuating strand of vibes. These people, unbeknown to most of them, were streaming like the river, innately moving from one sweltering spot to another, or much like salmon, to the end of some instinctual destination. He surely hoped, though, it was not their demise, but then, he surely possessed the power to prevent such and would, at all costs.

They buffered against one another, looking at him from across a pebbled street in their t-shirts and summer dresses, some hoisting and squeezing several rubber rats that had found their way well beyond the hall. Overall, the people stared at him, sensing his aura, in addition to his renowned prestige, anticipating he would speak to them, but at such a far stretch, would it matter?

The voice inside, however, told him to follow through. He then halted, letting the words channel from his throat:

"I know we face a problem, my friends," he said, his voice traveling like a ventriloquist's, deftly readjusted and thrown. "One sector of our town tips an insidious way, while the other holds its ground, hoping to stop the onslaught. Trust me when I say, we will stop this festering scourge." His brain bristled, more words brewing. "Though these past few days have felt like years, tonight I foresee that matter will be settled. Yes, it will be either us or them, and you know as well as I, that in this battle between good and evil, there is no chance these connivers will win."

In an uproarious sweep, the audience cheered, but in the backdrop, beyond the many avenues, his expanding mind sensed the Guaners hunkering, their legion marching, some even robed. He saw punches thrown, heard derisive names called. A few blocks down, Charlie… jabbering a mile a minute…gathered more gents like himself, so that they formed a brigade, fists formed, set to fight.

"In our hearts, we know violence is a last resort," Mansford continued, his words now feeling more like his own, "but we've reached that point of no return. We've no choice but to harness all that we hold precious. We have to push back at the source…at this charlatan called Gyler…expose him for who and what he is." He felt an intense, a cerebral hiccup ready to break, but for the moment, restrained it. "We nearly revealed his true colors last night. Now we must finish the job. Now we must—"

The pages of Pickwick's book once more flashed, passages flickering through an array of paragraphs, until the following entry lifted: *If a sacrifice should ever fail or miss its scheduled designation, Guaners may revamp the designed twofold, conducting rituals simultaneously. This may bolster success, thus embittering and confusing their enemy, and if by chance one sacrifice should falter, then another may at least reach fruition, for even those pure in heart may find it difficult to occupy two locations at once.*

"We must expose the full extent of his villainy," Mansford cried. "We must march to the heart of the city, where our adversary resides. We must thrive through our wisdom…our piety." He clasped his hands as if in prayer. "Please believe in what I say, for this is the only way to win. I have attained the insight to ensure this win. I know what to do…where to go."

A telepathic camaraderie permeated through the people, then swung back to Mansford. Phil Sutton felt it, too, tottering from its thrust.

"Whoa…you feel that, Mike?"

"Yeah. Consider it a positive sign that things are swaying our way."

"Okay. So, what now?"

On the surface, Mansford was uncertain, but in allowing his instincts to spark, he deterred the question and instructed, "For appearance sake, I'll head to the car, make it appear I've boarded, but head out on my own. Take Carl and Ned with you. Lead the people onward. Get somewhere between the museum and library, then mingle…clear your head, get something to eat, drink, call your wife if you want. I'll meet up with you soon enough."

"Meet up?" Sutton was perplexed. "Geez, doesn't sound like much of a plan."

Mansford grabbed his arm and clamped it. "Trust me on this, Phil… please."

Sutton winced, pulled his arm free and nodded.

Mansford moved toward his Packard, inspiring people to follow. One even tugged the back of his coat, remarking, "It worked, didn't it, Michael? I mean, the good word sure spread."

He turned and regarded Father Bruno's beaming face.

"Look at all the people," the father continued, looking most regal in his priestly best and widened his arms. "Miraculous, indeed, and to think it started so small, so unassuming, a mere sprinkling of friendly chatter, and then…"

Mansford's heart sank, for he recalled the children's kidnapping.

"What's wrong?" the priest asked, noting Mansford's glum expression.

"Nothing, Father," he fibbed. "I'm just in a hurry, as I'm sure you can well understand. Listen, I truly can't thank you enough for your efforts." He pointed to the car. "Why don't you accompany the other fellows?" He shot his keys to Sutton, while motioning Clive and Stark nearer. "Trust me. We'll finish this. I promise."

The father looked puzzled but soon grinned, the crowd flowing closer. Mansford then ducked, pretending to board but ambled onward into the mounting, twilight mist, his pores burning, his body and clothes dissolving, transforming, as the mask snuggled his features like a clump of warm clay.

"*Excellent,*" said the voice within.

He then ascended: a star-like flicker, slick and swift.

(XXVII)

The people trekked onward, following the Packard, though some tracked the obscure specter in the sky, linked and nurtured by its magnetic draw.

The buildings beckoned the Persona: two mocking, squat towers of mortared brick, formidable and impenetrable in their aged stance.

"So, they're preparing," he commented.

"Definitely," his Persona side replied.

"And the people," he observed, "they'll cover the entire strip before long."

"Yes," agreed the magnanimous voice, "though the Beguiler's cronies will be waiting in the wings. Already, more than a few melees have erupted as such."

"We'll keep pushing our way in…outnumber them."

"Indeed, we shall, but our strength mounts not from quantity, but through our faith."

The two personalities formed one, unruffled wavelength and discerned a series of heavy croaks. They detected new beasts snapping, stretching, while those already hatched continued to develop, their human aides layering their foul gunk, chanting to ensure the hideous procession continued.

From a shadowy spot, Poindexter emerged, not far from where Sutton had parked the car, a mere half block from City Hall.

The mayor flailed about and stammered, "Oh, dear…oh, dear, what's happening? Where are the police? We must maintain order. We must."

The Persona could not have agreed more, especially when two visions rose in each of his transcending eyes:

The first featured Standish, robed and hooded. Other hooded characters accompanied her, climbing stairs, clutching sharp, little stakes.

The second featured Murphy, still gagged, his face streaked with sweat and fear. Another group of hooded fiends accompanied him, also ascending with their shiny stakes…

"Indeed, two locales," the Persona assessed, penetrating the steamy fringes the Guanars had erected. "Interesting, but I wonder…which is which?"

Grunts and groans, along with some spirited cursing, broke below, causing the Persona to insert his back-up eyes, and through Mansford's gaze, he saw Charlie and his brigade confronting a young group of Gyler supporters.

"Alas, it appears," said the Persona, "that no sooner do we mesh, we must again part."

Mansford's psyche crumbled, though only enough to understand his other half's intent. He let his molecules separate from his spiritual imprint and like a lightning bolt, snapped at the ground, his mortal sustenance reforming, though this time sans the mask.

Charlie sensed his presence and turned. "Say, there…it's Mister Mansford." He stepped from his troop. "Hey, Mister Mansford, I spread the word, just like you requested. Didn't think it'd come to this, though, but don't worry. We're prepared. I'll have you know, more than a few of my pals here fought in the Great War."

"I'm honored to know that." Mansford watched Gyler's thugs approach. "Now, I don't want anyone to get hurt. Maybe you can keep them preoccupied with a nice, philosophical exchange, Charlie…that is, just distract them, if you will."

Charlie shrugged. "Whatever you say, Mister Mansford. Sure wish I had held onto my lunchbox, though. It would have come in handy for whacking these youngsters over the head."

"You damn fascists," an older man yelled at the youths. "We don't want your kind in this town. Go to some dictatorial regime where you belong."

"Poindexter's the fascist," a young rough countered. "He's part of the old regime, the one that keeps the rest of us down. The sooner we get rid of him, the better."

"Who you kiddin'?" another older gent yelled. "What do you know about being kept down? A little jerk like you probably never even worked a day in your life."

"Ah, blow it out your hole," another teen bleeped. "We're takin' over this town. You geezers are through."

This lead the opposing sides to start slugging, with Charlie in the forefront, his arms twirling like a couple, unhinged whirlwinds.

Mansford popped his dagger from his pouch, poised it upward, hoping to ward off those who foolish enough to approach.

"Stand down," he commanded. "Hear me? Stand down."

Stark, Sutton, Clive and Father Bruno pushed toward him, prepared to pound anyone who even dared assail their benefactor, but when a couple young snots lunged at him, Mansford dispelled them each with the blunt brunt of his handle, while guiding the blade toward another couple of youthful oafs who crept from the side, raising blades of their own.

"Go on, lads," urged Mansford. "Test your luck...if you please."

Perhaps there was something in Mansford's pasty scowl, a glowing remnant of his higher counterpart, that made the boys hesitate. Whatever the case, with only a few threatening sweeps of his dagger, he prompted the boys to reel across the street, where they merged with another flood of Gyler's beady-eyed thugs.

"This is gonna get nasty," warned Stark, positioning his fists.

Clive approached. "I dispatched my reporters, but I'm sure they've been swallowed up in all the hub-bub. Still, we've got to document everything that transpires. When the dust clears, people need to know."

"The hell with that," grumbled Sutton, stumbling inward, his eyes energized despite his haggard posture. "Let's crush the opposition. That's all that matters." He looked to Mansford. "I'm sure you've got more than the means, Mike."

Mansford relished his friend's logic and focused ahead, while the celestial part of him gazed upward and said, "*Stay with it while you can. We'll reunite when the moment is right.*"

No sooner had these words saturated Mansford's mind that the brawlers pounced, delivering ample road-house blows, but the amicable opposition fought with heartfelt conviction and none more than Mansford, whose spontaneous dexterity shot a hundredfold, thrashing his assailants, slapping their ears, nicking their rears, even severing their belts from their pants when he could, leaving them straddled.

The fighting continued a while longer, until Poindexter's supporters seized the upper hand, pressing upon their weakening, younger counterparts. A familiar voice growled its advice.

"Settle down," the Great Beguiler cried, standing between Rothstein's Kosher Deli and Timmon's Dress Shop. He stepped forth in his wrinkled work clothes and shared a long, flustered frown. In fact, he was not more than twenty feet behind Poindexter, who had landed several effective uppercuts to a few brawny brawlers.

However, it was, in fact, these pugnacious types...Gyler's typical, doughy men of varying size...who snuck around the mayor, leading the remainder of the Guaner patsies to form tight clusters, their eyes fixed upon their guru. Then, the ersatz dwarf and middle-man tossed the anticipated crate before their leader, and upon such he leapt.

"My poor misled citizens," he pleaded, "fighting is obviously not the answer. Why should we lower ourselves to their zealous level? The only reason the financial elitists strike is because they're frightened...frightened we'll seize from them what is rightly ours...their shops, their cars, their money...which given time, we will nonetheless acquire. As much as we crave that ambitious goal, we must be civilized...make others see as we see...believe as we believe."

A few hateful hisses came from Poindexter's gang, while the mayor regarded his tormentor with shoulders thrust forth: the bruised Father Bruno and Sutton set themselves to the left of him, the battered Clive and Stark to the right, with bloodied Charlie surfacing from the rear. One and all, they proudly embraced their sentinel stances.

Mansford, meanwhile, gazed up in hopes of his spiritual consummation, but in so doing, detected a large, shadowy shape lodged between the deli and tailor: its eight, long, clawed limbs braced between each mortared side, so that it resembled a giant spider.

Indeed, it was the true Beguiler, smug and uninhibited as it gawked, emulating the Persona's symbiotic dichotomy: perhaps more to imbalance his adversary's mental state than cause him any physical harm. That the creature could simulate such a stunt, while yet projecting the manipulated semblance of humanity, prompted Mansford to point his blade at it, in hopes that others might be made aware. Of course, it was only he...and his heavenly offshoot...who saw the demon.

"At all costs," the projected Gyler puppet said, "I must become mayor, so that I may spread our humble, revolutionary creed to others in need. I need you to spread that word for me, even after I win my station, so that our cause can better extend to other locales, eventually covering the entire nation."

Mansford moved closer toward the beast, unsure what he would do upon reaching it, only knowing he had to approach, his frustration mounting when he realized the behemoth had begun ascending, propelled quickly by its many clinging claws.

"For now, go home, good people," the puppet ordered. "Let us spring our peaceful challenge another day. Let me investigate the highs and lows of our mission, reassess any points where we've gone wrong, and maybe in the process, unravel the whereabouts of that poor officer, see if he still resides among us...and we surely hope with our collective hearts that he does...for once he uncovers the corruption, we can further catapult our campaign."

With an instinctual bounce and a beckoning draw, Mansford's mind re-aligned to its higher vantage. Through the Persona's perspective, he awaited the monster's arrival, but as the beast's beady eyes met his, it formed a wicked grin, dissolving like a great, black storm cloud, spewing erratic sparks, before fading somewhere unseen.

"It's best we go home now," the puppet finalized, its voice now small and faint. "Get your rest. Tomorrow we carry on...but peacefully, honorably, assured we will expand our league."

Into the distance, the Persona stared, capturing the library in one eye, the museum in the other, meticulously peering through each facade, each roof, combing each level and corridor, but when he failed to detect his adversary, he drew his attention back to the separate stations of the Chaotic Command.

The Gyler projection vanished, with the original reassembled separately inside the buildings, all the while maintaining a symbiotic link as they rose: one via the library, the other the museum, but which harbored which?

Atop the library, the hooded Pascale pushed open a panel and climbed out, his hooded compatriots close behind and somewhere in the their midst, the gagged Murphy emerged, pushed hard and dropped like a sack of potatoes.

Pascale opened a large, brassy canister, circled the putrid gook around, retraced it for good measure and then squirted lighter fluid onto it. His comrades purred and muttered in curt, foreign tongues, at which time the Persona deciphered them.

"Accept this sacrifice, oh, Lord of Infinite Darkness," they blabbered, one over the other, "this pillar of society, who abides by the law, who restricts what we can and cannot perform. We will cut him to pieces, defile his purity and set what is left aflame. We will burn this temple's collection of knowledge, erase each and every foundation of each and every social confine, so that chaos reigns supreme."

Pascale tossed the containers to the side, generating a couple ominous clangs and paused a few feet from the squirming officer. He removed his hood, looked to the stars and scoffed at their grandeur. He then pulled a bright, clean stake from his pocket, as the others closed in, raising their own above their heads, awaiting the time to strike.

In a flash, the Persona descended, churning a wind so impetuous that Pascale and the disciples bumped and tripped over one another.

With the dagger pressed within his gloved hand, the Persona snipped Murphy's gag and intended to lift him, when his vantage bounced back to the museum rooftop, where another gathering had formed, including Pickwick, Standish, the gray-haired woman, and alongside them, four children: two boys, two girls.

"Please help," Murphy beseeched the majestic shape. "Please…whoever you are."

The Persona severed the remainder of Murphy's bonds, allowing him to crank upward, only then to be knocked back down by prevailing wind, which in turn inspired Pascale and several smelly goons to tackle the poor man.

"Slash him," Pascale commanded. Punching and kicking, Murphy tired to break free from them. "Cut off his finger…better yet his entire hand. We'll send it to the authorities." He then shook his stake at the Persona and laughed. "This silly angel can't stop us. Hell, nothing can. The Great Beguiler has so ordained it."

The henchmen positioned themselves to slice, but the Persona swept down upon them, and with one mighty sweep of his hand, hurled them from the roof.

Panicked, Pascale charged into another dizzying cluster of subordinates, tripped onto his knees, scooting under their robes, dropping his stake and reached into his robe for a match.

With a sadistic sneer, he struck it, his eyes fixing on the Persona's icy countenance, which began to fluctuate, mirroring his own.

Years of Pascale's torment and frustration surfaced, searing through the Persona's consciousness like a slew poisonous spears. In merciless droves, the Persona reflected the vile emotions back at Pascale, forcing him to re-experience his bumbling years as a renowned cheat with the dark and absurd. He chocked on his desire to destroy the world, confused by why he would ever resort to something so meaningless and drastic?

Perhaps, he had no place in it, at least while it harbored potential good, yet in the midst of this misguided perception (and through the Persona's astute reinterpretation) he realized how he had missed the obvious. Only through others had he opted to wallow in misery. He had fallen for their lies, having become too obstinate, too lazy to propel his imagination, to dare to dream and hope to believe in the simple, miraculous joy that could be culled from so many aspects of life.

The foul circle burned. Robes caught fire. People shrieked, groaned. Unnerved by the sight, Pascale grabbed his chest, his heart halting. The flames reached what was left, rolling across his carcass like a great, orange ball.

Despite Pascale's collapse, several hooded fiends found the courage to lunge at the mystic, but with a wide stroke of his blade, he pricked them and in so doing, they tipped like bowling pins along the fiery rim, their agonized cries curdling into the air.

The roof then began to crack, its concrete breaking in large portions, but how…why?

Perhaps such was a result of the sinful concoction, with the results worsening per the flames. The Persona, however, had no time to decipher the causes and effects and soared, circled, exuding a breezy, ethereal mist, which extinguished the fire and vaporized the fluid, solidifying the cracks and indentations, erasing all signs of the calamity. He then grabbed Murphy's hand.

As the subordinates writhed, or in confused agony, leapt to their deaths, the Persona enshrouded Murphy with his aura, escorting the officer upward and onward. All the while, he focused on the museum roof, pulling it ever nearer in his mind, his aura moving in so fast that it felt as if he had been stationed there the entire time.

"Amazing," the spellbound Murphy exclaimed, as the Persona placed him onto the new location, behind those gathered. "Thank you, whoever you are, for saving my life."

The Persona nodded, but also turned his attention to Pickwick, who now sprung toward him, cocking his spike.

"Oh, I know who he is," the High Monarch snarled, his eyes projecting bright, preternatural insight. "It's the King of Avarice, playing with our minds. So, how did you do it, Mister Mansford? To what prissy entity are you in league?" He slowed, but pumped out his chest. "You must know how ridiculous that pliable countenance looks. Twist and turn it all you desire, but I assure you, it'll never achieve the desired effect."

Despite Pickwick's brash declaration, the Persona stayed silent, looking beyond his foe, focusing on the stoic Standish, the children huddled around her, as well as the minions moving in.

There was pugnacious Butch, the gal who had accompanied him off the bus, his pudgy friend and the Schwinn girl: all too close to Mansford's heart, and therefore, of course, the Persona's. They appeared arranged to be spread upon their backs, and though they tried to look unafraid, their underlying tension seeped, which was only expected, considering the number of spikes directed at them.

The Persona also noticed, within the extinguished circle's heart, the Guaner museum sculptures centered, as well as the old book and at various other spots along the ring, piles of old, ruddy spikes, used on victims through centuries past: their cumulative vibrations strong, tainting the air with impending doom.

The Persona again regarded Pickwick, his followers continuing to press inward, staring at their patriarch, then at the children…up at the Persona, then back to Pickwick. Standish, meanwhile, grew more rigid, appearing like a mannequin, with the shadow-faced woman moving nearer, her head cocked, as if about to whisper.

"You're outnumbered Mansford," Pickwick proclaimed, saliva layering his lips. "You might as well face the fact; we've a bona-fide army here. Yes, granted, you're fast…indeed, far faster than I could have calculated, but not fast enough to prevent us from fulfilling our task. The duality of our stations delayed you, as prescribed." He pointed at the children. "Putting those precious darlings in harm's way has struck the right chord. They're ours now, and their deaths are guaranteed to rival that of a meager policeman, let alone a fair-haired virgin. How will you live with yourself after these lovely children have perished, when you know their collective demise sealed our victorious fate?"

Pickwick looked satisfied and maintained his steely stare. However, unbeknown to him, his true thoughts had entered the Persona's head, like angry waves crashing against the shore, and soon upon his white, glassy face, the misguided man's emotion beamed and within the menacing sheen, various chunks of Pickwick's memories formed.

"No," Pickwick murmured, twisting in anguish, "no…don't do this to me. It's…it's far too hard to accept…too hard to remember…"

The Persona perceived Pickwick's days as a woeful, young man garbed in tattered clothes, aspiring to be something grand, working his way through school, gaining a scholarship, attending college, learning about worldly topics, traveling, collecting, landing his first job, rising within the museum's ranks, becoming its curator, but with this illustrious goal achieved, despair followed. He felt trapped and alone, until—

She appeared: a bit mature, but no less attractive for it. She was independent, with that glint in her gaze that said no man could ever own her. She sauntered through the museum aisles, inquiring on those obscure, historic periods few ever acknowledged. She seemed desperate for a companion, despite the ring on her finger and admitting to having an infant. She even denounced her vow…indeed, the type of woman he was looking for, and when she proclaimed that the world they knew should perish for its hollowness, there was no turning back.

She referenced forms of Aztec poisons, their undetectable aftereffects, said she wished her husband was dead, and if so, she might marry someone else, with whom she could explore the arcane, perhaps conceive a son somewhere done the line, teach him to despise sentimental traditions, in a way she believed her current child never could.

"She…she simply told me her husband had died," Pickwick said with a regretful sigh, "a heart attack, you see, and though I knew of the poisons, I believed her, or maybe deep down, I just didn't care." Pickwick's lips quivered. "I had no choice in the matter, I suppose, anymore than I do now. She never did give me that son. It was all a lie, but I let it be. I always let it be."

This abrupt confession made the flock bristle. Its members regarded one another in bewilderment, shrugged in despair and lowered their spikes.

(XXVIII)

Little did they realize, another dreary presence had formed, its distorted features now existing as one.

A sooty aura had seeped from the concrete and merged with the oily residue and slinked like some great, dark ghost, emitting a dense, dizzying stink.

The Persona studied the hybrid's features: one sparking, plasmatic vein webbing out from the another, poking from either side like angled swords inside a magician's prop box, but they didn't stop there. From their tips, translucent tendrils yet rolled and flapped, reaching well beyond the roof… stretching their spectral limbs all the way to the library, in fact. People both good and bad lingered, some prodding the fallen bodies below, wondering what terrible thing might strike next.

The Beguiler laughed, its head still that of the phony Gyler, along with a slither of pale chest, which bled down into a black, fuzzy abdomen. Its outstretched limbs were more muscular than before, but with thick, monstrous wrists capped by wiggling, human fingers, and from out its bulky ankles, stubby white toes.

The Persona also then noticed that several translucent tendrils had latched around Pickwick's limbs, one even suctioning his neck, piercing the center of his throat, thriving with increased color with each passing second.

"I…I…never wanted it to…to…go this far," Pickwick stammered like a broken automaton, but the Beguiler squinted its two, little, human eyes hard and with its flimsy fingers yanked the man's throat vein, readjusting his voice to blurt, "Nevertheless, Mansford, you're still fighting in vain." It made Pickwick crack a grin. "Nothing good ever comes from good. Disorder is order, and chaos, the only guaranteed form of everlasting peace."

The Persona grimaced, shifting his gaze from Pickwick to the Beguiler, to whom he acknowledged, "You mean, much like what's happening overseas…where sadness and madness reign supreme?"

"Yes," it made Pickwick confirm, "Just as in those lands where foundations are being torn asunder, then reassembled into disorderly order…all without consequence. Indeed, if it can work there, it can work here."

"A bold presumption," said the Persona, looking again to Pickwick. "If not for being scared and suppressed, many of these people would dispute your claim." He peered deep into Pickwick's petrified eyes. "Come now, you know I'm right, Mister Pickwick."

Pickwick trembled, as the demon began to resume control, but found enough strength to scream, "Yes…I know the fear all too well. I won't succumb. I won't…not anymore."

Sobbing, Pickwick flung himself toward the Persona, his hands clasped in a nod for forgiveness, skidding onto his knees, and while most of his subordinates looked on in shock, two sprung at him, each grabbing an arm, hurling him back, their hoods bouncing off their heads, revealing their battered faces…Fred and Pete.

The Persona sighed, somewhat disappointed he had not detected their presence sooner.

The Beguiler laughed…a snide, little human laugh.

"I've grown weary of stodgy ole' Jon Pickwick," he croaked. "Besides, he's more than filled his purpose."

The tendrils dropped from Pickwick's shivering frame, the one at his neck popping like a cork. However, the Persona saw several others attached to Fred and Pete: finer, less radiant, but like those that straddled Pickwick, growing thicker, brighter.

Pickwick sensing his liberation, once more leapt toward the Persona, who in turn, widened his coat, swooping forward to blanket the frantic man, when...

Another hooded shape jaunted, prancing around Standish and the children. Her slender hands grabbed onto Pickwick's back, swinging him beyond the Persona's legs...and straight off the roof.

Pickwick's blood-curdling scream filled the air, then the sound of him landing atop the Blessed Tiding's truck.

A simultaneous gasp shot through the flock. The children's jaws dropped, and with a manic flutter of her lashes, Standish stirred.

The one responsible for Pickwick's tumble turned, revealing brilliant, translucent tentacles extending through her robe. Her hood slid off her gray hair, revealing her red-smeared lips and clownish smirk.

"Mother, my God," Standish gasped. "Mother...what have you done?"

The woman turned, and through her shallow cheeks, hissed, "Don't call me, Mother. If the truth be known, I disowned you no sooner than you were born. I only ever kept you the sake of sacrifice, no more than a potential pawn. Better would things have been if I only had a son."

Then like a mad marionette she leapt toward the children, swinging her spike at Butch, but the Persona...as if to compensate for not having thwarted Pickwick's death...bolted, his dagger severing the spectral links. With this, Standish's strands also fell, and she gasped in glee for having been set free.

Meanwhile, the pale-faced Beguiler flexed its fingers, and from its tips, elicited another slew of plasmatic strings onto the woman, with which it could control her gestures.

"Very well Mister Mansford," the old woman cackled, as the Beguiler twitched its lips, "very chivalrous, indeed, but as you can see, your fate is already sealed." The Beguiler waved an arm, and so did she. "As you can see, the plasmatic lines can stretch to eternity, and once this nation is laced with enough of them, they'll link to those beyond the seas, beyond the continents. We'll spring from one spot to the other, our generals transporting in a wink of an eye, giving their commands, harnessing the meek masses." The monster made the woman cock her thumb toward the rigid, stone-eyed Fred and Pete. "Neither the innocent nor the naive will escape our grasp. The entire world will fall victim to our incessant, chaotic blast."

The Persona darted toward the female marionette. The surrounding subordinates backed away. Her daughter cuddled the children, while a bleary-eyed Murphy stood, doing his best to flank them.

"Unlike you, Marjorie Standish," the Persona stated, "most don't aspire to be a puppet on a string, to mouth another's words, to think another's thoughts. For most, autonomy can never be bought, and for those who think otherwise, the consequences always prove dire."

The woman paused, severing the demon's draw. "I chose this outcome of my own free will," she said. "It was my choice...and my choice alone... to play Jon for a fool, Carmine Pascale and my daughter Stacey, all well... all my choice, my innermost desire. I orchestrated every last ounce of it, lurking in the shadows, whispering in their ears, planting the seeds of discourse, never letting up." She gave the hybrid an affectionate glance. "I summoned the Great Beguiler, to grant entrance in this restrictive world, and in thanks, the mighty one blessed us with human form, always promising the best of both worlds with only my precious loyalty in return." She glared at the Persona. "And what could the result of such an allegiance be?" she asked, looking with distaste upon her daughter. "Well, it's quite simple, you see. The Great Beguiler and I both savor the same madness. He loves me, as I love him, and as you well know, love...even of a dark variation...has no boundaries."

The Persona raised hand as if to strike her, but instead forced her chin toward him and searched her eyes. She blinked and croaked with the demon's intonation: "I know what makes you tick, Mansford. I've grazed those places where you've roamed, where you alter-ego has flown. I've learned a few mind-over-matter stunts as well, not the least of which is teleportation. When I was hiding, transported among the streets in hopes you wouldn't detect me, I perfected the skill with expertise. In fact, at this point, I'm confident I can administer it far better than you."

The Persona scoffed, and the demon stomped, springing its strands across the roof, which bannered the air like a burst of gossamer snakes. Marjorie Standish, however, embraced the role of puppet well, reaching into her pocket, grabbing her stake and cocking it back. Her mesmerized ranks followed suit and wasted no time to near her daughter and the children.

The Persona glided toward them, but the Beguiler met him head on, causing the two to thrash: flesh dicing flesh, soul searing soul.

Meanwhile, from out the fetid ring, the Beguiler's malformed minions mounted, but from their sides and hips, extra limbs emerged: dark, sinewy and horribly clawed, within seconds spewing from around the Beguiler's hide.

The Persona, however, ripped into the demon, not only with his dagger, but with keen cognition, forcing his glowing head up through the

…his dagger severing the spectral links…

Beguiler's throat, its radiance striking through the beast's large, buried jaw, making the false head atop it tip.

The creature's pseudo orbs caught its opponent's gleaming countenance, then the beady eyes behind these decoys focused. The Persona's moon-like countenance darkened as the beast's various eyes mirrored upon it.

A spurt of weakness overcame the Persona, but despite it, he conveyed, *"There's one thing you haven't yet mastered. You can't see the gamut of what I harbor, but I can see every vile ounce of you."*

The Beguiler croaked, but its fear permeated its need for resistance, fanning out across the roof, past the subordinates, who either cupped their faces or swatted at things they wished not to see. Their flooding panic found its way into the elder Standish, who scratched and clawed at the air, until she screeched, turning catatonic, as though caught in Medusa's hideous glare.

The grand expanse of the sky inundated their minds, lit by ancient images: helmeted men on horseback, grasping swords and spears, war cries curdling from their throats. Some were dark and brawny, others multi-limbed, all descending upon women, children...unarmed men. Blood spurt from their necks. Hope drained from their hearts, and village after village, into other skies of other times, they persisted their attack, with more misguided people following, dying, flayed on makeshift alters by sharp spikes.

The clouds moved. The stars quaked. Years passed, capped by the brisk thuds of goose-stepping feet, and through these militant sounds, fiery patches emerged: within them the purgation of a million words, a million artifacts. In their place, a mad aura reigned. Hopelessness spread: the past dead, but also the present and future, replaced by an endless stream of tears, fears and emptiness.

The Persona absorbed it all and forced it back upon the demon, aiming his hateful eyes into his opponent's equally hateful eyes, tossing all its crazed aspirations back onto the beast.

The twisted dreams shattered, leaving the Beguiler not only to croak, but scream, extending the sound so that it filtered through the throats of its disciples, then into its hooded rabble, rolling like dust across the roof, again igniting the odorous circle.

Cloaks caught flame. Men and women raced about, tearing off their garments, but their efforts were in vain, their flesh darkening and blistering.

The doughy men began to melt, their projected flesh flaking off in clumps. Their frames shrunk, their limbs cracked, until they were reduced to soot.

The confused Beguiler spat the Persona out from its moist husk, hurling him toward the ledge. The Persona paused, then hovered, his face phasing from black to white, his multiple eyes settling back into two, his lips turning soft pink. He regarded his bloodied dagger and grinned.

Standish and Murphy blocked the children from the maelstrom, the former keeping a eye on the mother, who then shook off her catatonia, craning her neck enough to catch her daughter's gaze.

The older woman swung her spike, but Murphy leapt up and kicked her in the stomach, knocking her back into Fred and Pete, who had waddled from behind to shed their tendril-shed cloaks, their eyes now clear. They grabbed the woman's arms and forced her down, glancing up at the Persona, their expressions begging for redemption.

The Persona soared, his dagger pointed behind them, for the ever diligent ex-dwarf and mid-man were crawling legless across the concrete, each stretching an insinuated claw at the caretakers' ankles, but Fred and Pete sidestepped the creatures.

The Persona reached around the men, slashing monster's necks. They slithered a spell before fizzling into slimy puddles, their muck stretching toward the hunkered Beguiler, which had abandoned its remaining, human attributes, slumped and drained.

The creature ambled a tad, sliding its body outward, its flabby jaw hitting the surface, its tongue lapping the repugnant residue, its sides heaving.

"The Great Beguiler will grow again," the older Standish threatened, twisting her body to break free, "the next time stronger, wiser...you'll see." She grew more incensed as the Persona landed before her, his ghostly face beaming of stoic sympathy, which enraged her even further. "You can never defeat its ilk, you pompous harlequin. It will only find passage back to its world, kill and devour until its belly is once more full. It will conjure a whole new bag of mental tricks, and when the time is right...when all of you holy buffoons are rested and content...my dearest, lustful consort will—"

In a roaring flash, the Beguiler sprung up and crunched its jaws down upon her. Blood spurt from her mouth, her eyes bulging in shock, her upper body breaking off.

Standish cringed and covered the girls' eyes, while Murphy shielded the boys. The Beguiler only snorted, continuing to feast, undisturbed by their presence, intent on appeasing its hunger.

The beast then looked downward, peering into the building, its heightening perception absorbing a great, gaping pit below. The beast no longer cared to defile the building's contents, let alone kill the children. It only wanted to crash through the foundation, plummet back to its dark, unearthly lair, where it could again grow strong.

The Persona could not allow this, and so when the beast spit out his ex-betrothed's fleshless arm, he leapt into the air, landing on the Beguiler's back, slipping his dagger deep into its bullish neck.

The creature reared up, its four, front paws scraping back and forth, bucking as hard as it could to toss its opponent off, but the Persona used his dagger as leverage, plunging it behind the beast's neck, giving him enough time to consume its confusion.

The flames mounted. More mystified Guaners tripped and faded. More humans jaunted, some yet leaping from the roof. The Beguiler then managed to throw the Persona from its back, causing his dagger to slip from its wound, out of his hand. The beast somersaulted with reckless grace past Standish and the children, landing in a balled bundle toward the ledge.

The Great Beguiler turned, snorted, and kicked backward, extending its limbs outward, and with a hateful snort, charged.

Standish and Murphy ducked, pulling the children down as the beast leapt over their heads.

The beast hesitated, began to reel, for much to its horror, the Persona had beaten it to the punch, having adapted its full, hideous form…a raging behemoth, fit and strong that sprung up, reached out and snatched the Guaner by the throat. The Persona clamped his jaw upon the creature's shoulder, deepening the dagger's wound, his glassy eyes growing electrified as he flipped his opponent upon its back.

The Beguiler squealed, fully aware of its mortifying fate, allowing its stronger, more vibrant counterpart to claw its chest and abdomen, yanking and scraping away all the budding strings, symbolically defiling all the evil the retched thing had ever conjured or savored.

The dying Gauner then blurt a final croak, its dissolving flesh spiraling up in an overlapping grid of smoke and stench, into which all similar elements then meshed, including the statues, spikes…text: the only pieces of the past, perhaps, worth extraction.

As the beast's husk dwindled, the Persona threw back his own knobby head, flapped his knobby arms, sending bloody droplets across the expanse, as he reverted to a serene, clean, human form, floating within the haze.

The eight survivors regarded him, uncertain what to do, where to go, but the Persona opened his hand, into which the dagger materialized and returned it to his hip, the pearly glow of his cheeks hardening, breaking from his skin, so that the mask popped from his face and dropped into his other hand, back into to his holster. He then asked them to gather near.

From out his coat flaps, an enveloping mist spread, anointing their pores, their thoughts.

Within seconds, they joined hands and above the doleful display, rose into the clear, unfettered sky. Though most of the horrid remnants were nearly vanquished, they could not help but acknowledge the broken bodies below: a profound reminder that, despite the surreal nature of their adventure, they could not dismiss the harsh reality of war.

(XIX)

The children skipped toward the Packard, oblivious to the unnatural circumstances that had brought them to this point, their quiet, astral descent now forgotten.

With open arms, Father Bruno ran and embraced them, sobbing joyful tears.

Ambulances were stationed in the near distance, their sirens silently swirling, as police sauntered toward the library, acknowledging the additional bodies, while other officers kept onlookers (many of whom had been Gyler supporters) at a respectable distance.

"There's a lot more bodies at the museum," Murphy called to them. "It was quite a scene, I must say…on both ends."

"Hey, that's Jack," cried one of the officers.

"Holy smokes, if it ain't," said another.

They dashed toward him, offering their hands, patting his back, bombarding him with questions, while additional officers followed, dashing around Fred and Pete, whose wounds had grown fainter by the time they stumbled toward the forefront.

From the side, Charlie surfaced, waving at Mansford and Standish, his eyes droopy, his attire battle-frayed, but in keeping with character, jabbered, "Hey, there, you two, what a night, wouldn't you say? Never seen nothin' like it. Would swear it was a dream, but whatever the case, at least our side came out unscathed." He wiped the blood off his chin. "Well, at least virtually so."

As Standish removed her robe, revealing a short, white slip, the old guard placed his hand on his heart and sighed, turning to Sutton and Stark, who had merged with Fred and Pete: each duo helping various ambulance attendants load the casualties. From there, Charlie swung his finger at Clive, who ambled over to accompany his elder counterpart, approaching the young couple.

"My buddy here's right," said the newsman. "Man, oh, man, what a night. The revolution's last leg rose and fell within mere hours. Murphy's back at least...hallelujah on that. The question now is: how in the world do we decipher this craziness, let alone report it? Hell, even the mayor seems to be muddling up his facts," he acknowledged, as the excitable Poindexter beelined by to converse with the gathering officers. "Doesn't make things easy."

Mansford grinned. "I say, tell what you know, Carl, as well as you can. That should more than suffice."

Clive frowned.

"Yeah, I guess it was only natural the details might fade," Mansford muttered, more so to himself, and glanced at Charlie, whose gaze seemed glazed. "Sure, you remember the basic elements, the ones that feel cohesive enough, but otherwise..."

"Elements?" Clive scoffed. "What feels cohesive, you say? Well, there's nothing normal about people indulging in fiery rituals upon rooftops and leaping to their deaths. I dread to think what else we might find. This Gyler creep seems to have financed himself a veritable suicide cult. That's not something one can easily shake. The only good that'll come of this is Percy's inevitable re-election, and of course, a lot of foolhardy citizens may have gotten a good wake-up call. Still in all, what a damn shame. No one deserves this sort of outcome, not even a bunch of lunatics."

"Perhaps," said Mansford, watching Fred and Pete hoist another body onto a stretcher, "but then, we do reap what we sow. I'm afraid this may be another grand example of that, Carl."

"Yeah," I suppose," Clive agreed scratching his head, "I suppose." and then he stumbled off with Charlie, who offered his own profound but grossly inaccurate speculations on the matter, the details of which were skimpy.

This prompted Mansford to march on, Standish close at his side.

"How are you holding up?" he asked.

"All right, I guess, at least as well as anyone else who's survived such an ordeal...whatever it was." She pouted, her eyes misting. "My mother...my step-father...they're—"

"Yes," Mansford affirmed, "they're dead. Pascale, too, along with a good number of other poor, misguided people."

"But why, Mike…why? I keep running it through my head, but I can't make myself understand, and now it seems so fuzzy, so elusive. Did it even happen? Did it, Mike?"

Mansford was tempted to rekindle her memory, to remind her of his other self, but sensed the sudden futility in such, which in turn made him wonder, was he also destined to forget?

"Who can say why things happen as they do?" he blurted, absorbing her tears with his gloved finger. "Who can say why people chose to do the things they do, when and if higher forces might intervene? It's not for us to reason why. We just press on, live our lives to the best we can and strive to do what's right."

Mansford realized the preachy nature of his response, but Standish accepted it and asked, "Can we get out of here, Mike? I don't want to talk to the police. I wouldn't even know what to say. I just want to go somewhere safe, secure." She glanced up shyly. "Your car's back there. Maybe we can go to your apartment. Maybe we can."

Temptation seized him, an overriding need to pull her near, and yet he remembered what Surrogate had said…yes, Surrogate, wherever he resided.

"That wouldn't be such a wise idea," Mansford responded, "though you certainly do need a place to rest." He regarded the police cars. "You've been through a lot, both mentally and physically." He removed his precious coat, wrapped it around her. "The hospital is probably the best place. I know you'd rather not, but perhaps one of the officers could."

"No, please," she begged, but as she rubbed her palms upon the coat's velvet trim, she hesitated and appeared more assured. "Okay," she said, "sure, if you really think I should."

"Indeed, I do," Mansford replied, leading her toward the officers, who were yet piling on Murphy.

It was agreed that she and Muprhy would both be escorted for a thorough medical check.

Standish handed the coat to Mansford before boarding the squad car, even though he insisted she still wear it, but once she dropped the garment into his arms, he acknowledged its importance and re-donned it. He then stroked her cheek and bid good-bye.

For a time, he milled about with Sutton, but he was more inclined to make amends with Fred and Pete. This led Mansford to chat with Stark, then Poindexter, who held on to the notion that much of the commotions had been caused by drunken brawlers. Last but not least, he met up with Father Bruno, who was most understanding, but also anxious to accompany the children to the hospital for a good once-over

Indeed, as Mansford had assumed, the outlandish events were becoming little more than one big blur. If anything, people thought nothing extraordinary had occurred, pretending to be impervious to the grisly remnants, forcing themselves to make small talk, letting the stranger aspects of that night sink farther into their subconscious minds, deep into those corridors where logic ruled over fancy. But the Beguiler's rise was anything but frivolous, and no one knew that more than Mansford, for the Persona insisted he would not forget.

He returned to his car, taking Sutton, Stark, Fred and Pete home. He then visited the cemetery, noticed the holes filled and smoothen, assured the alteration was more than an illusion, and felt a tad better inside.

Nonetheless, the early-morning atmosphere proved edgy enough to keep him moving, thinking, recalling, and again impulse took over, leading him to the dock and to the smoky-faced specter who awaited him.

●●●

"It sure took you long enough." Surrogate skipped across the planks. "Don't get me wrong, I'm most at home around the water. Still, I expected you hours ago."

"Sorry." Mansford approached him. "I had to sort my thoughts, figure things out…then I got the strange inkling you might be here."

"Nothing strange about inklings. You'd be best to savor them. You're one of the few in this town…heck, in this entire world…who can."

Mansford stopped before him, his expression taut and serious. "Why's that?"

"You know very well," Surrogate had plumes spurting from the sides of his mouth as he tried to repress a smile. "It's because you were plucked, and it was no accident that Marjorie Standish and her Chaotic Command chose Blessed Tidings to summon your opponent. It was destined that way, but of course, it was your own choice to tackle the onslaught before it worsened." Surrogate patted Mansford shoulder. "I'm proud of you, son. With only one exception along the way, you performed remarkably well, which is more than most of your global counterparts can say, but even among those few who have made the grade. You've rivaled them all."

"Which means?" asked Mansford, the mask vibrating against his hip.

"You're becoming a guardian," Surrogate explained, "a noble hybrid of man and deity… just like me. Oh, you may not believe it, but I once played your part, even though I'm best known by an earlier name and a more legendary occupation." He raised his finger. "Go on. See if you can guess."

Mansford smiled and shrugged.

"It's Simon…Simon Peter, to be exact," Surrogate confessed, the smoke billowing in thick gushes off his face, "better known as Saint Peter, a fisherman by trade, an apostle of Christ, and of course, sentinel of the holy gates." He pointed to Mansford's hip. "You don't think the mask, and all the wisdom it carries, came by accident, do you? The Lord would never have allowed the gates to be tinkered with, unless for a virtuous cause, and the result you presently possess is the very one I once wore on my various sojourns…as well as several good men thereafter. Yes, indeed, Michael Mansford, you're part of a very long, prestigious legacy."

"I'm flattered," Mansford said "though I wouldn't have imagined being up to the task. I mean, despite some luck, what makes me rank so high? I did slip, you know, and if I did it once."

The smoke was gone from Surrogate's face, revealing the saintly persona behind it: a strong brow and jaw, a distinguished mustache and beard.

"Because," said the elder statesman, "I was able to see, and all along the path, only once did I sense anything that went contrary to my belief, whether I was acting as the proverbial fly on the wall, or staring through the eyes of your friends. Oh, yes, I've occupied more than a few of them along the way, if only to observe the proceedings…Sutton, Stark, Clive… Father Bruno, he being most recent in that honorable track. That's what my new job entails, you see. I keep an eye on things, but rarely intervene. It's ultimately up to the general participants to decide what course they wish to take, which often comes down to blind faith. Of course, once in a while, they're granted a fleeting revelation to help with a particular cause. Such comes, goes, and if need be, your friends will remember again, if ever trouble strikes. Nonetheless, it's essentially up to those special few to make things right, to help maintain the good things in life. By trade, Officer Murphy understands this…and does Father Bruno…and the rest…and on the same ethereal level, so do you."

"I guess," Mansford patted his hip to douse the vibration. "I feel different, though. It's hard to explain."

Saint Peter smiled. "Sooner or later, each of us evolves. You're just doing it quicker than most, abetted by your all-too-human, child-like quirks. It all goes to reason, though. The mastery of god-and-man is a hard one to nurture, but it clicks, despite the apparent contradictions, and though you're a minor case-in-point within the grand concept, in the end you'll more than make your mark. You entered a most significant scenario, fixed it accordingly, but there are other tricksters yet to come." He winked. "Trust me. You've only just begun."

Mansford was at a loss for words, daunted by the realization that such a mythic responsibility had been laid upon him. What did it all mean? How far along would it go? To what extent would he, in fact, continue to evolve?

Saint Peter sensed his concern. "Don't ruminate on the matter to much, son. When the time is right, you'll know what to do, and as for everyday life, well…you don't have to be a choir boy, either. Now, I'm not saying you should indulge in every salacious activity that comes your way, but there's nothing wrong with a spirited courtship…if that's what you desire. A man of action generally hungers for such and now that the young lady has been, well—"

"Deflowered," Mansford offered.

"More or less," Saint Peter smiled. "Nonetheless, a good man will make amends, and just as the dear Lord well knows I fell and yet repented, you, too, will come through."

Mansford nodded, hoping he was up for the lengthy task and assumed he should request further advice, when the saint backed up and waved.

"Should be shoving off now," he explained with a sideways glance. "Just wanted a moment to cap things off face-to-face…in a nice, personable place." His countenance started to haze. "It would be wise to try to enjoy your newfound occupation. Make the mask a symbol, an emblem to embody your intent, like the Lone Ranger…Zorro…or if I may be so bold, me." The smoke swooshed inward, enveloping his face. "Besides, a disguise always keeps people on their toes, even if by chance they do discover who you are." He rose. "And remember when it comes to your patrolling, never dilly-dally. Remember…evil always works behind the scenes, in shapes both big and small…ever vigil to take advantage of those foolish enough to wait."

Mansford ran after him, his feet teetering on the dock's edge, watching as his majestic mentor entered the clouds and like a fleeting spark, faded away…

Mansford walked back to his car, mystified but contented, the vibration of his hip continuing: a reminder of what dwelled inside him, confirmation that, as he had known all along, he and the Persona were meant to be as one.

EPILOGUE

Mansford kicked his way through the autumn leaves in his floppy trench coat, eager to reach the theater. He paused upon spotting the trash receptacle, atop which the pages of the latest Brink Town Times fluttered open, revealing an ad for Esoteric's latest sensation: The Creepy, Clutching Hand.

Smiling, he lifted the edition and the front page: PENELOPE JAMES TO WED TEXAN TYCOON...POINDEXTER REMAINS UNCONTESTED...PERSONA STRIKES AGAIN—HALTS ASSAULT.

He focused on the latter:

"A senior was spared an unsavory outcome in stately Primrose Square Friday night, when an adolescent knocked her to the ground, attempting to steal her purse. Fortunately, the individual known to Brink Town residences as the Persona, intervened by thrashing the suspect. After such, he reportedly swept the young man away, delivering him to beat officer, Jack Murphy, to whom the alleged assailant confessed his intent, claiming the mysterious vigilante had not only probed his mind, but had stolen his face."

Mansford chuckled, continuing to read, but a sudden tapping interrupted him.

He glanced over, saw Standish sitting a few feet away, in her little ticket booth, a kerchief-less gag rat squashed alongside the register. She smiled, motioning him closer.

He tossed the paper back into the receptacle and dashed over.

She looked at ease, as was the case since her position had become full-time. Saturdays, though, were long, with the kiddie matinees, capped by a main feature.

"Early as usual," she pointed out. "But I'm glad." She fought back a yawn. "Thank goodness my shift is almost through. I'm quite tired, Mike. Would it be all right if we just skip the movie tonight and you walk me straight home?"

"You sure? After all, we're talking 'Adventures of Robin Hood' here."

"As I recall," Standish countered, "we saw it during its premiere. This is a re-release, you know."

"All the same, you know how much I fancy those flamboyant do-gooders."

She rolled her eyes. "I'm not scheduled for work tomorrow, so perhaps we can catch the early afternoon slot…after church, that is."

"Sure."

He waited until her replacement arrived and then escorted her to the boarding house where she now resided, not far from the park and a decent stretch from Primrose: the library and museum well out of sight and therefore, out of mind.

She stopped upon the first step, looked into his eyes.

"I'd ask you in, but a male visitor wouldn't go over well with the land lady."

"I know. It's perfectly fine. I mean, what can one do?"

"I suppose, we can enjoy each other's company when we can," she suggested, "savor those special, little moments we have." She giggled, extending her hand, displaying her shiny engagement ring. "The girls at work are so jealous. They said you have a good eye for jewelry, but then, you ought to, being the resident dandy."

Mansford laughed. "Hey, you're the one who picked it out."

She blushed and shoved her hand inside her pocket. "I have a little something for you, too." She fluttered her lashes. "Would you like to see?"

"All right."

Out of her pocket, she revealed a roll of white fabric and unfurled it until it touched the ground.

"Well, what do you know?" he grinned. "A scarf…how lovely. Why thank you, my dear. It's much nicer than my black one…a lot longer, too."

She wrapped it around his neck, flipped and curled it. "Thought it might come in handy with it getting colder, but it's more for looks than anything else. I know how you like to hob-knob about. It could even be effective when you, well—"

He searched eyes, discerned her suspicion.

"Yes, it'll embellish the rest of my attire when I, uh…make the rounds."

She reached over, kissed his cheek and skipped up the steps. "See you tomorrow, Mike. We'll have plenty of time to enjoy each other's company…I promise."

"I'm sure we will," he watched her enter the house, his yearning strong, but restrained. "Tomorrow it will be."

He then sauntered onward, inhaling the autumn air, glad to be alive, in love, and oh-so-intuitive, especially as he neared the Brink Town Bank and watched the unassuming, black car roll into the lot.

He heard the voices of the stocking-faced men inside, assuring one another that this was when the employees counted the money. He watched the hoodlums leap out, their weapons poised, creeping toward the back door.

He shed his outer coat, exposing his Edwardian garb, slipped on his gloves, snapped his holsters, grabbed his dagger and of course, his trusty mask.

Now as the Persona, he rose, coat and scarf flamboyantly flapping, his mind open wide, his majestic form aimed fast.

THE END

An Appreciation

My love for the pulp icon adventures goes back to when I was a mere lad, commencing not so much with the printed word, but rather the repeats of old-time radio shows I would listen to on Sunday afternoons in the '70s with my dad. The likes of the Shadow (who projected the same mysterious appeal to me as the Batman) and the Green Hornet (of whom I had already become a fan from the '60s television show) made strong impressions on me. Also, the Lone Ranger, Flash Gordon and Tarzan figured significantly into the influential mix.

Over the years, my sense of right and wrong has been strengthened through these programs, as well as their offshoots: comics, short stories and movie-serials, including those featuring Captain America, Captain Marvel and Superman. In these current times, when bad is often mistaken for good and vice-versa, or criminal acts are greeted with apathy, I have come to relish those older forms of entertainment and their noble content perhaps even more than ever before.

In fact, "Enter—the Persona!" was born from my yearning for the past and the morality that characterizes it. In real life, I could not pull a Don Quixote (the original, literary avenger, if the truth be known) and sally forth to right wrongs. However, I could use my imagination to pacify my woes, and what better way than to set my philosophical fancies in writing: create my own superhero of sorts and relegate him to the time-frame of those heroes my father appreciated.

My character, Michael Mansford, aka the Persona, is really the embodiment of one who takes an ethical stance. The character has a dash of Christian mythology tossed in him, but I would hardly call him or my story religious or comparable to, let's say, Bibleman. Mansford is a far cry from a choir boy, in this respect, and his mortal content (equipped with all the flaws that any man would have) surfaces even when he becomes a masked crusader who, in this case, absorbs the bad deeds of those he hunts, only to toss the sting of their criminality back in their faces. (How's that for teaching the cretins a lesson?)

The Persona also abides by the Steve Ditko philosophy of distinguishing good from bad. To say there are shades of gray in the Persona's approach would be erroneous. On the other hand, there is also a fair sum of wild psychedelia that distinguishes his make-up: Lovecraftian, I suppose, but still Dikto-esque, or Dr. Strange-eseque, when one comes down to it. Indeed, the Persona can slip into some weird, far-out channels, even though his mortal self is relegated to a straight-and-narrow '30s perception, particularly when it comes to matters of life and justice.

The story's prime villain, the Great Beguiler (aka, Ben Gyler), projects the pretense of being a commoner, an "everyman", even though he is the antithesis. He and his disciples (some demons and some misguided humans) intend to trick the masses (or at least those of little Brink Town, NJ) into following their insidious lead. This is a reflection the Nazi propaganda that was successfully plaguing Germany around the time my story takes place.

Mansford knows the Great Beguiler is nothing more than a silver-tongue devil, but how does he (or more precisely, the Persona) get people to see through the trickery? The exposing of evil has been a concern of mine for quite some time, and I believe it's something that concerns many of us in the current scheme of things: how do we get closed-minded people to care that there is a difference between the extremes?

Well, I hope you like my story and its hopeful message. You may just find that the good ol' Persona represents you as much as me, and if so, I would be most satisfied. If you wish, you can touch base with me at http://bizarrechats.blogspot.com/ or simply feel free to email me at mikehousel@hotmail.com. I would be ever pleased to hear from you.

ABOUT OUR CREATORS

AUTHOR –

MICHAEL HOUSEL - Over the years, has penned horror, science-fiction and psychodrama short stories, as well as reviews for toy and hobbyist periodicals. He is also the author of the monster-rally novel, "Flask of Eyes", published by Caliburn Press. You may visit his blog at http://bizarrechats. blogspot.com, where he offers reflections on a variety of fantasy-based topics. You can email him at mikehousel@hotmail.com.

INTERIOR ILLUSTRATOR –

ART COOPER - is a Canadian artist/writer/editor who was a founding partner of Spectrum Publications, which published three bi-monthly fanzines in the early '70's. Art was a member of the inaugural Cartooning program at Sheridan College in Oakville, Ontario, where the guest instructors included such luminaries as Joe Kubert, Neal Adams and Will Eisner. Art contributed to a number of fan publications and penciled two stories for Orb Magazine before getting married and completing his engineering degree. Art has worked as a project manager in the Mining and Metals industry for the past few decades, and has done some freelance advertising work on the side. Art is the proud father of two grown sons, and lives in Mississauga, Ontario with his current wife and daughter.

COVER ARTIST –

SHANNON HALL - Shannon Hall is an artist of many mediums. He grew up watching his dad paint in the traditional medium so there was always a great love for all forms of art in his household. Shannon's love for comics and illustration was inevitable and so started his journey into the world of Super Hero and Fantasy Art. Shannon is best known for his work on such comics as "Angry Citizens", "Mr.Cynic", "Lance Star", and several yet to be published anthologies. He also continues to try and "break in" to the comic industry. Until then, he continues to seek out other creators and collaborate on future projects.

http://shannonh.carbonmade.com
shameous@bellsouth.net

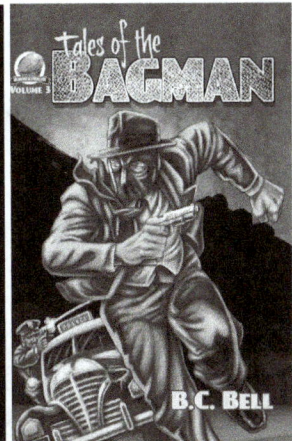